DATE DUE			
MAY 26 '00	DEC 30 '00		
JUN 22 '00	JAN 18 '01		
AUG 12 '00	FEB 10 '01		
AUG 21 '00			
SEP 1 '00	MAR 05 '01		
	APR 5 '01		
SEP 6 '00	APR 13 '01		
SEP 11 '00	MAY 01 '01		
SEP 29 '00			
OCT 16 '00	MAY 10 '01		
NOV 07 '00	JUN 29 '01		
NOV 25 '00	JUL 06 '01		
DEC 26 '00			

4 / 00

JACKSON COUNTY
Library Services

HEADQUARTERS
413 West Main Street
Medford, Oregon 97501

DESIGNING WOMAN

DESIGNING WOMAN

Vera Cowie

This first world edition published in Great Britain 1999 by
SEVERN HOUSE PUBLISHERS LTD of
9–15 High Street, Sutton, Surrey SM1 1DF.
This first world edition published in the USA 1999 by
SEVERN HOUSE PUBLISHERS INC., of
595 Madison Avenue, New York, NY 10022.

British Library Cataloguing in Publication Data

Cowie, Vera, 1928–
        Designing woman
        1.   Love stories
        1.   Title
        823.9'14 [F]

        ISBN 0-7278-5421-6

Typeset by Hewer Text Ltd
Edinburgh, Scotland.
Printed and bound in Great Britain by
MPG Books Ltd, Bodmin, Cornwall.

DESIGNING WOMAN

One

"Three months!" Harriet's voice soared off the scale.

"At the very least," her doctor confirmed.

"But I can't possibly leave my business to run itself for that long!"

"Then find a temporary substitute."

"*Harriet Designs* is a one woman operation and that woman is me."

"Then you must make it your business to find a clone." Inexorably: "You need a complete break from work, Miss Hilliard. You are underweight and, from what I can see, under par. My diagnosis is overwork, resulting in extreme stress and borderline exhaustion. What you need is rest and recuperation in a place as far removed from your shop as possible."

"But I love my work!"

"To the exclusion of all else, it would seem – and there are a great many other elses. One does not live to work after all."

I do, Hariet thought mutinously. She thrived on it; always had done. Piers Cayzer, her silent partner, said she consumed it as other women did chocolates, except she never gained weight. On the contrary, of late she had lost it, and rather too much: fifteen whole pounds. But I am NOT ill, she refuted inwardly. I am NEVER ill. I

1

can't remember the last time I was unable to function through ill health. Piers says I have the constitution of a horse. 'A thoroughbred', he always added with a proud smile.

"Surely you can find someone trustworthy to take over for three short months," her doctor was insisting. "What about Mr Cayzer?"

"He is my silent partner," Harriet said abstractedly. "He provided the financial backing I needed to start up on my own, but he knows nothing about interior design. I run *Harriet Designs*. I AM *Harriet Designs*."

"But you must have staff, an assistant—"

Harriet thought of Miss Judd, her right (and left) hand, but only insofar as administration was concerned, and of Evelyn, her secretary, much younger but equally capable in the handling of clients and suppliers. Reliable and relied on both, they were nevertheless in no way interior designers. "Neither is capable of running my business."

"Then you must look elsewhere. This is a matter of urgency, Miss Hilliard. Either you rest or—"

"Or what?"

"A complete nervous breakdown. The human body can take only so much and you have been taking the whip to yours for far too long. The fact that you fainted is a warning."

"It cost me a pair of Louis XVI *fauteuils*," Harriet said aggrievedly. "Just as I was about to make the clinching bid."

"Surely your health comes before a couple of chairs?" her doctor rebuked. "You badly need a complete break and I suggest a cruise. Right away from everything to do with work. Somewhere tropical,

2

where the sun shines every day and you can take advantage of it; carefully, of course and with the proper sunscreen. If you do not, then I must warn you that you are liable to find yourself forcibly incarcerated in a clinic."

"Surely not!" Under her protest Harriet felt a stab of fright.

"Oh, but surely yes. You are obviously wound to snapping point. All work and no play is every bit as bad as all play and no work. There is a happy medium and I suggest you find it as quickly as possible."

"But three whole months!" It was a moan of pain.

"At least."

"Couldn't I work part-time – say, five hours a day? That way I could keep an eye on things and rest at the same time . . ."

Her doctor's expression had her voice fading. "You said that last year when you came to me to complain you were not sleeping. I suggested you trim your workload then, and did you do it?"

Harriet shifted in her chair.

"What is happening now is a continuation of what was happening then. Had you heeded me I would not need to be so strict now, but you ignored my warning. While the work is there you will immerse yourself in it; we both know that. Which is why I want you distanced from even the temptation."

"But I am right in the middle of a most important commission! I've done the designs but I must stay and see the work carried out to my satisfaction."

"No."

In a flare of exasperation: "Then tell me where on earth am I going to find the sort of stand-in I need at

3

such short notice? People like that don't grow on trees."

But Piers, when she despaired of the possibility at some length over dinner that night, stunned her with surprise when he told her he knew exactly where one could be picked at her leisure.

"Talk about fate! I know the very man. Absolutely perfect for your needs. He is a very old friend of mine, just back from New York where he was with Lewisohn's – and aren't they just about the biggest in your particular field?"

"As huge as their commissions – entire hotel chains, vast Arab palaces and such-like. *Harriet Designs* is very small fry compared with that!"

"James can work small as well as big – has done, in fact. He took a Fine Arts degree at Cambridge – got a First, too – and Sotheby's snapped him up in a flash, then after about seven years with them he went to the V&A and it was from the museum that Lewisohn's enticed him to America. He is the answer to our prayers, darling. Top notch, is old James. He'll take care of everything for you." But Harriet's aquamarine eyes were sparkling in a way that had Piers' heart sinking. He knew that belligerent light; it always shone when there was a threat to her heart's darling. He was well aware that the thought of leaving it to fend for itself for any reason was anathema; to leave it to the tender mercies of a perfect stranger was the stuff of nightmares. She had worked long and hard to get where she was, single-handedly at that, but she was a demon for work. Still, even now, punishingly ambitious; always wanting just that bit more. But he could be equally determined when what he wanted was at stake.

"James has all the right qualifications; more to the point he has the time and I am sure he will also have the inclination once I have explained things to him. He has the very best of helping hands, as I have good cause to know. He has come back for a sabbatical anyway—"

"Are you saying that running my small business will be a holiday?"

Piers hastened to mend the hole his foot had made. She was so infernally touchy these days. "No, no, of course not! All I mean is that it is . . . fortuitous . . . that James should have returned to England at this particular time. As you say, it would have been a herculean task to find someone to stand in for you at such short notice. He is the proverbial gift-horse, darling. Why must you insist on examining its teeth? Take my word for it, James is the answer to all your prayers. He is a whiz at what he does."

"I have not done so badly for myself," Harriet reared, stung.

"Of course you haven't – you have done incredibly well in ten short years. But didn't I know you would the very first time I set eyes on you, when you came to see me full of the most ambitious plans and not a penny to back them with?"

"Every penny you lent me has been repaid, with interest!"

"That," Piers reproached, Christopher Robin eyes filled with hurt, "is the least of my worries."

Harriet gritted her teeth. Her silent partner was not a forceful man, but he had his sticking point when it

5

came to financial acumen. She knew that sulky set to his mouth: it meant hurt feelings. Oh, do grow up, Piers! she thought impatiently. Sometimes he came the sulky child too much; every time he looked in the mirror he must practise his "little-boy-lost" expression, aided and abetted by the thick sheaf of silky fair hair, the blue eyes, the rosy cheeks. He was forty, not four. She did not realise that her own hectic flush and high-voltage eyes betrayed her inner turmoil as she apologised tiredly: "I'm sorry, I seem to be burning a very short fuse nowadays . . ."

Piers seized his opportunity. 'Because your doctor is absolutely right: what ails you is nervous exhaustion, and I am bent and determined that you will follow his orders and take a nice restful cruise in sunny climes, far away from this awful February damp and cold. It will bring you back to me with the spring, and I promise you that old James will have everything running on oiled wheels when you do."

"You make him sound like the Second Coming," Harriet observed crossly.

"As far as you are concerned he is a miracle!" Piers responded, tart as a lime for once. Reaching for her hand he coaxed: "You'll like old James. Women always do. He's a handsome one. A real charmer—"

"My shop runs on a great deal more than good looks and charm!"

"Oh, he is no dilettante, make no mistake. He is as capable a fellow as you could ever find. If you were to comb the head-hunting agencies they could not come up with anyone so perfect for our needs."

Our needs? was Harriet's response, still not in the least impressed. Nobody was good enough for what

6

she had laboured long and hard to create. Leaving the light of her life in the hands of a stranger made her blood run cold.

"Why don't I bring him round for a drink tomorrow evening?" Piers suggested. "We are lunching together so I'll put the idea to him then and if it appeals I'll bring him round and you can size each other up, ask him the all questions I know you will want to raise." But he could see that Harriet was far from convinced. Really, he thought, it is becoming harder and harder to insert the thinnest of blades between the two Harriets. If something is not done soon they will merge. He had always been aware of her ambition, but she had got to the top, hadn't she? Why would she persist in trying to add to the height of the mountain? Picking up her other hand, both of them fine-boned and slender, like the rest of her, he held them between his own. "Don't you think you are – identifying – rather too much with the other Harriet?" he asked, treading very carefully. "It makes me uneasy, this obsessive zeal of yours. You should be relaxing after your triumphant climb, not making plans to scale the next peak. Look at you; pale as a corpse and thin as a wand. It won't do, darling. You have lost that lovely apricot glow of yours; you are short-tempered and irritable and it worries me. Please, my love, step back and take a good look at what is happening to you. All work and no play is making you into a very crotchety lady".

Harriet felt a pang of dismay. She knew she was not looking her best – had not for some time now; knew people trod warily in her presence these days. But she had not realised that Piers, not the most perceptive of men, had noticed so much. Trouble was, he was a fusser, and because fuss irritated her she tended to turn him off.

"It is as though all your lights had been dimmed," he was complaining. "You never seem to relax. Your reputation is made yet you are always prospecting for the next client even when your order books are full. We don't go out nearly as much as we used to because you say you can't spare the time." He paused. "We don't make love as often as we used to either, because you are always tired. It troubles me to see you looking so drawn and – dare I say it? – almost haggard . . ."

Not a vain woman, Harriet knew a sudden impulse to rush to the nearest mirror. Haggard? At thirty-one? She put up a hand to her cheek as though expecting to feel ridges and furrows instead of the still flawless smoothness she looked after so carefully.

Watching her, Piers pressed his advantage. "You are all shuttered, your radiance dimmed. Please, darling, do take this much needed rest and recuperation."

"I am not some shell-shocked soldier," Harriet protested, but the conviction in her voice had lost its strength.

"And neither is James your enemy. Why, oh why are you so reluctant to accept any sort of help? You and that precious independence of yours! Just remember that if you go on working an eighteen-hour day you will lose everything – including me!" Startled by this uncharacteristic display of firmness, Harriet could only stare as Piers went on: "You are to go away and leave all your worries behind. Soak up the sun, eat lots and lots of lovely food and get all those enticing curves back. Rest assured that James will keep an eye on everything. He has the sharpest of eyes."

Of a most unusual colour, Harriet thought when she met them for the first time the following evening, so dark a blue as to be almost inky black but with an added iridescence, as though the ink had a mercury base. He was also big. Piers stood five feet ten inches in his stocking feet and was stocky with it; James Alexander topped him by at least four inches and out-weighed him by forty pounds.

She was at once very much *aware* of an intense physicality; of the heft and breadth of powerful shoulders topping a broad chest and narrow waist, with a long length of leg below. He had very thick, very glossy, just tending to curl dark hair, worn rather longer than Piers' conscrvative short back and sides; in fact just clearing the collar of his beautifully cut crisp pale blue shirt, which went perfectly with the elegance of his navy blue pinstripe. She could have applied her lipstick in the shine on his shoes and she caught the gleam of sapphires in his heavy silver cuff-links. A dandy! she thought disgustedly. Much use he will be! Devoting time to his appearance instead of to *Harriet Designs*. Harriet distrusted men with male-model good looks. She had been warned – times out of number – by her mother about handsome men. But over-riding the good looks and the charisma Harriet was instantly aware of one, very salient fact. This was *not* the kind of man you would ever call Jimmy.

"So you are Harriet Hilliard," he observed inter-estedly, in a voice that would have given Richard Burton a run for his money, the mercury eyes una-

9

bashedly eyeing her up, down and sideways. "I have heard so much about you from Piers – all in the most flatteringly prejudicial terms, of course."

Harriet forced herself to stand still under his comprehensive scan, seeming to probe behind the Jean Muir-Estee Lauder partnership. As always, she was neat as a pin down to the last eyelash; nape-length, ash-blonde hair blunt cut so as to fall into place with a couple of strokes of the brush, a pair of extravagantly lashed, aquamarine eyes of remarkable brilliance and lustre set in a translucently pale skin, and a sculpted yet luscious mouth with a full lower lip and enchantingly short upper one. This was somewhat compressed as she met his probing gaze with an inimical one of her own, but as he towered over her five feet four inches she was obscurely glad she had chosen to wear a favourite suit in her favourite French navy, the high collar of its jacket concealing the salt cellars which had recently emptied at her collar bones even as its long jacket hid her weight-loss. At the same time its colour enhanced her own.

As their eyes held she caught their gleam and realised with a frisson that in James Alexander she was being presented with a Challenge, but since all her life she had enjoyed meeting – and beating – them, her smile was glittering as she answered sweetly: "I am afraid you must make allowances for Piers' . . . enthusiasm."

"How much do you want?"

Oh, yes, Harriet thought, metaphorically curling a lip. Pure brass. Up to every trick in the book because he wrote it. Gift of the gab, calculated charm and no scruples. Instant and instinctive dislike made her say, with almost palpable insincerity: "It really is too kind of you to consider helping me out like this."

"What else are friends for?"

The way he returned her insincerity with interest confirmed that she had a fight on her hands. "Please, do sit down," Harriet invited politely. "No doubt Piers has told you what is expected?"

"Oh, Piers has told me absolutely everything."

That last word made it clear that Piers had made a Full Confession, but though Harriet gritted her teeth she forebore to flash her eyes at him, standing by beaming at them both, tickled to death by his own cleverness.

She sat down in her favourite chair; an old *bergère* in fruitwood, upholstered in slubbed silk the colour of ripe strawberries, back straight, ankles crossed, hands folded, while James Alexander bestowed his long length onto the Victorian sofa she had rescued at a country auction and re-upholstered to match the chair.

"Have you seen any of my designs?" she enquired.

"Lots, and admired them all. The Harriet Hilliard style is unmistakable."

"I'm flattered," again, with patent insincerity.

"So am I, to think you are willing to take me on sight unknown."

"Piers knows you, and I trust Piers."

"One can always trust Piers," he agreed, but in a way that again indicated to Harriet that the kind of trust he meant was not the one she had in mind. He had a way of saying things which spoke added volumes. "He has helpfully given me chapter and verse."

Harriet knew what that meant. Piers tended to wax rather lyrical where she was concerned and while she

11

was happy to let him take pride in her, she was not about to have James Alexander mocking it. Instinct was telling her it would not do to give this man any kind of leverage; he would have even the Walls of Jericho toppled before you could say "fire". I don't know what it is but I don't like you, she thought, and I would not trust you as far as I could throw the Eiffel Tower. Something about him raised every hackle she had yet she knew she could not afford to tell him to get lost, because other instincts were telling her that he was as good as she was going to get at short notice – amazingly good, in fact. Behind the charm, not to mention that infuriating insouciance – yes, that was the word – insouciance, she sensed there was both the knowledge and the capability she was after.

"I appreciate how difficult it must be for you to go away and leave your business in the hands of a stranger," he was saying sympathetically. "Piers tells me you have never left it for more than a week before, not in all the ten years you have been building it up?"

"Nor would I be doing so now unless I was being forced to," Harriet answered, flinging a rancorous look at her lover, who admitted cheerfully:

"She can't stand even the thought. Harriet is a demon for work. It is all she ever thinks of."

Raising silky black eyebrows: "Surely not," James Alexander murmured.

Again the underlying implication made Harriet livid but she ignored the jibe and stared him down. "Are there any questions you wish to ask me?" she said crisply.

"Lots."

"Then by all means ask them."

12

Which was when she had to admit that he knew his business. Every question was one she would have raised herself. It was obvious he already had a very good idea of just how her shop functioned – Piers had left no *i* undotted, no *t* uncrossed – nevertheless she gave him a complete run-down on the way things stood: commissions in hand and their various dates of completion; fabrics on order, suppliers used, craftsmen employed, deliveries promised, starting dates to be kept. It was finally agreed he would come into the shop to work alongside her until her sailing date was fixed, which, according to Piers, would hopefully be within the next ten days or so. That would, James said blandly, enable him to 'get the hang of things', leaving Harriet in no doubt as to what he would really love to get the hang of. Of all people, Piers had to come up with a womaniser. Which was when she had her idea.

"There is one particular job I would like you to give special attention to . . . a very important client. Her name is Harcourt-Smith. She has bought an Eton Square penthouse and I've done the designs, which she says she loves, but she keeps trying to slip in bits and pieces of her own which will ruin the whole effect. She has a very great deal of money but her taste is MGM musical. She hooked her first millionaire while she was in the chorus of *My Fair Lady* and she tends to sweet-pea colours and chiffon. If she is allowed her way the penthouse will end up as a cross between the set of *Sunset Boulevard* and a New Orleans bordello. I should be grateful if you would curb her wilder excesses while allowing her some leeway, always ensuring she does not try to slip one – or more – past you. She is up to every trick in the book . . ." Like you, her look said. "Work is due to start within the week, so if you could monitor it – and her – closely . . ."

"I will make it my priority."

As she will make you hers, Harriet thought gleefully. Sadie Harcourt-Smith was a maneater. Three husbands, each one richer than the last, and a grip like a moray eel.

"By the time you return she will be eating out of my hand," James promised.

If you've still got one, thought Harriet vengefully.

"Well, didn't I tell you?" Piers enthused. "Isn't he perfect for your needs?"

"It's his needs I wonder about. What is all this going to cost me, Piers? Nothing was said about how much. He obviously comes dear and I don't see why I should squander my hard-earned profits—"

"It's all arranged," Piers overrode in the voice he used when discussing money. "You are not to worry your pretty little head about it. I have taken care of everything – no, I will not tell you how. I may be your silent partner but I am a partner and *I* am dealing with this, not *Harriet Designs*. You forget, James is an old friend; he is doing this as a favour to *me*. It is therefore my responsibility to see that he is adequately compensated. That is all you need to know."

You mean all you are willing to tell me, Harriet thought, but she was touched nevertheless by his concern, as well as relieved not to have to foot the bill. She had not the slightest doubt that James Alexander came anything but cheap, and so when Piers indicated in his diffident way later that he would like to stay the night, she made no objection. It was the least she could do, she thought guiltily.

On the following Monday, to Harriet's chagrin James Alexander took over without a shot being fired. On being introduced to Sadie Harcourt-Smith he had her not only eating out of his hand but eyeing him hopefully for crumbs. Even Harriet's own devoted staff laid down their arms, and she had no doubt that Evelyn would have laid down a great deal more had he so much as raised an eyebrow, while Miss Judd, not given to praise, said approvingly once she had his measure: "That one knows his business, Miss Hilliard. You should have heard him dealing with Latham's. I could not have done it better myself." The ultimate accolade.

Over the next ten days Harriet watched and learned what was meant by a Smooth Operator. He charmed the clients, soothed the suppliers, mollified the manufacturers and whipped from under the nose of Harriet's keenest rival a Sheraton commode she thought she had lost for ever.

The night before she sailed, dining *à deux* with Piers, he asked her confidently: "So old James is doing well, then?"

What do you mean old? Harriet thought irritably. He can't be a day over thirty-eight. "He knows his job," she admitted. "I'll give him that."

"But nothing more? I can't understand why you don't like him, because you don't, do you? I can feel it when you are together; the atmosphere positively crackles." He shook his head. "I've never known it happen before. Everyone likes James. He is a most likeable fellow."

15

Harriet shrugged. "*Chacun à son goût.*"

"Well, I am sorry he is not to yours, and that's a fact. Still, all that matters is that he does right by *Harriet Designs*, eh?" Piers chuckled. "Mind you, James never normally has trouble with women. At Cambridge he cut a swathe through Girton, Newnham – all the women's colleges." He paused. "As a matter of fact, it was through him I met Paula."

Harriet stared. Piers evaded her eyes, moved his shoulders uneasily, pink cheeks pinker than usual. "She was very keen on James, you see . . . but he was not so keen on her. As a matter of fact he warned me about her—"

"Before or after?" Harriet enquired nastily.

"Oh, before . . . he always said she was on the make."

"Well, she certainly made a fool out of you!"

Harriet could have bitten off her tongue at the look on Piers' face.

"That was unforgivable", she apologised instantly and unreservedly. "You are right. I do need this break."

Piers' face cleared. He knew Harriet was not normally vicious. "You have every right to tell the truth," he admitted gallantly, serving Harriet fresh pangs of guilt on a bed of frustrated irritation. "She did fool me. I was quite – besotted. Since I met you, of course, I know it had nothing to do with love. I took her at face value. I am afraid I don't have James' ability to see beneath surfaces."

"Well, hers is pretty dazzling," Harriet said, needing to atone.

"Yes, but like James says, all surface and no depth. I took her gilt to be what you are – pure gold." Reaching

16

across the table he picked up her hand, kissed it reverently. "You are so patient. All this time you have waited and never complained. I don't know what I can have done to deserve you."

"Had faith in me, supported me, encouraged me – and lent me a great deal of money."

"Lending money is my business and you were a gilt-edged investment. No, I was not thinking about our business relationship. I meant us."

Harriet said nothing. She knew Piers thought a great deal more about the "us" side of their relationship than she did, but as always, when he talked about it her little demons of guilt got out their tridents and started prodding. She was very fond of Piers; she had promised to marry him hadn't she? When (and if) he obtained his freedom from a wife who was in no hurry to let him go. She shared his bed whenever he wanted her to – which was not all that often because Piers was neither highly sexed nor a particularly skilful lover, which suited her because her own sexuality was set to Low anyway. Piers approved (and was not a little relieved) by this; he thought it proof of her 'ladylike' qualities. Paula had been sexually voracious and he unable to cope, which was why she had taken up with men who could satisfy her, knowing that Piers, with his Edwardian ethics, would never go so far as to admit to the world via divorce proceedings that he had a serially-adulterous wife who had cuckolded him more times than he had fingers and toes because he could not bring her to orgasm. This reluctance on his part meant that Harriet, who was quite content to let their relationship hang in limbo, could give all her time and energy to what really mattered to her: *Harriet Designs*.

Lately though, she had noticed that Piers was beginning to chafe at the bit. Not surprising since it was almost four long years now, which meant that he had another year and a bit to go before he could have the discreet divorce he wanted: the five year separation, the all-done-through-lawyers-no-publicity-sign-here-please kind.

Piers had every last one of his class's phobias, not least a horror of public notoriety. Like his peers – his older brother was one – he was unconcerned as to what went on inside his social circle but ultra-sensitive as to outside press reports. Paula was always appearing in the glossies, but only in the social sense. The thought of appearing in the scandal-greedy tabloids brought him out in a cold sweat; so did the even more hideous prospect of Harriet appearing with him, since Paula was quite capable of counter-suing on account of his own adultery, thus hoovering up large tracts of the Cayzer fortune in alimony. Which was why it had been a long time before he hesitantly made any approaches to Harriet which she, deeply grateful as she was to this man who had financially made what she craved possible, did not rebuff. It was, she had thought, as she always thought where Piers was concerned – the least she could do.

Now Piers said: "I think, while you are away, I really will see what I can do to light a fire under Paula. I don't think I can bear to go on for yet another fifteen months."

"Then why have you let it?" Harriet asked, with the confidence of one who knew only too well. "Sixty years ago your attitude was still the done thing. A gentleman did not divorce his wife for adultery; one

allowed her to divorce you. Times have radically
changed, Piers, so have the divorce laws. You could
have divorced Paula for adultery a dozen times or
more since I have known you; your private detectives
have furnished you with plenty of proof – yet you
prefer to wait five interminable years for the no-
names-no-fault-irrevocable-differences kind."

"I find the thought of being involved in a public
wrangle most upsetting," Piers replied stiffly. "You
know very well there has never been a divorce in my
family, nor the merest hint of scandal come to that. I
was raised in the school that says a gentleman never –
but *never* brands a woman publicly."

"Paula has been wielding her own brand in private
for long enough," Harriet reminded brutally.

"But with circumspection."

"Which is why she will never divorce you, in spite of
you having left her."

"I am aware of that, but if she will agree to a quiet,
unpublicised divorce now, I am prepared to make her a
decent settlement."

"What is decent to Paula is indecent to everyone
clsc. She won't go quietly, no matter what the circum-
stances, unless you pay her what she thinks she is
worth. She is quite prepared to dive into the biggest
pool of publicity she can find if she thinks it will help.
What you need, Piers, is a replacement; one rich
enough to make her drop you like a hot potato."

"That would be a dirty trick," Piers reproved.

"How many has she played on you? You are too
forbearing. Don't you ever feel the need for a little tit-
for-tat?"

"What good would that do?"

19

"It would give me a great deal of pleasure, for a start!"

"You are much tougher than I am," Piers admitted, "though one would never think so to look at you."

"You are extremely tough when it comes to money."

"Ah, but that is different. One has investors to consider."

"Haven't I invested in you?"

His smile was loving. "And I will protect that investment always . . . I will never allow Paula to brand you, never."

"Then we are back to square one."

"Are you so tired of waiting?"

"I told you back at the beginning that I was prepared to wait," Harriet side-stepped.

"Which is what I find so amazing. That a woman who can be devoid of patience when it comes to her work should be a veritable monument to it where I am concerned."

Only because it suits me, Harriet thought guiltily.

That night, Piers departed, saying, "No, I won't stay tonight, darling. You need rest after these hectic ten days. James takes a deal of keeping up with, I know. Once you are your old self again then I will love you as much as you wish, but for now, let me show you I can be patient too . . ." He kissed her tenderly, then left, leaving Harriet to finish off the last of her packing. Piers had used his clout to get her, at short notice, an A-deck suite on a cruise liner in whose company his family's bank had a financial interest. But as she carefully folded trousers and shirts and dresses in sheets of tissue paper, she found herself thinking for the first time in months – years? – about the situation she and Piers were in; one she had come to take for granted.

When she first met him, it had been as an ambitious twenty-one-year-old straight from Goldsmiths, toting a newly acquired BA(Hons) in Design Studies, and a relentless ambition to become the foremost interior designer of her day; a combination of the two Davids – Mlinaric and Hicks – and Nina Campbell. To this end she had approached – since she had been told he was approachable – Piers Cayzer of Cayzer Uhlmann, merchant bankers who specialised in venture capital. She'd heard he had a reputation for backing outsiders who had then gone on to win some pretty important races. He received her courteously, listened at first politely then with rapt interest to the naked ambition expressed in the form of scrupulously detailed and flawlessly concise plans issuing from the face of an angel. If wishes were horses then this flower-faced young thing was already in command of a regiment of cavalry, so he had backed his hunch and backed her, his every expectation proving to be justified. What he had not expected was to fall in love with her.

Piers was already much married, having done so in great haste which he went on to repent at every leisure moment. Paula Ames had been the Face of the Year when he met her, pursued by a great many men. Naïve as Bertie Wooster, and totally inexperienced as to the wiles of the gold-digger, Piers had been dazzled when she chose him, so blinded that he was totally unable to see that it was not him but his money she wanted, and he had a very great deal of that.

Paula had come up the hard way from Chingford, starting small with a minor rockstar and progressing onwards and upwards from rich man's hand to richer man's hand. Using their money she had re-made herself, spending it on elocution lessons, health farms, plastic surgeons and *haute couture* until she had the drawl of a Chelsea deb and the appearance of a well-brought-up gel, all of which evaporated once she had his twenty-carat engagement diamond and matching pure platinum wedding ring on the third finger of her left hand.

The marriage Piers thought dreamily had been made in heaven turned out to be an ante-room to hell. Paula was never at home and he soon found out that it was because she was in somebody elses, always the property of a man. She spent money like she had been given a finite time in which to do so, and when he attempted to remonstrate told him with Chingford honesty that she had to have some pleasure in life since he had not the slightest idea how to give her any in bed. But she was careful. She had no intention of ending her marriage; it was too gilded a cage and there was never any shortage of brilliantly plumed males willing to share it with her. Once she had the measure of Piers' phobias she ceased to care. The front was kept up at all times, but behind it was a swathe of adultery. It was not until after meeting Harriet and falling in love with her that Piers found the courage to leave the house in Hill Street and move to his club, leaving Paula to play the discarded wife, protesting vociferously that she had no wish to end her marriage; that Piers was welcome back at any time.

When he knew he wanted Harriet as a life partner as well as a business one, he told her the truth about the state of things, and asked her to wait for him until such time as he could arrange an amicable, discreet divorce. Harriet, who was as deeply grateful to Piers as he was in love with her, said she quite understood and was prepared to wait. That waiting had become as much part of the relationship as everything else and Harriet now found herself contemplating the fact that she never really believed Paula would let go.

Gossip always had Piers in a blue funk, so while he courted Harriet and took her out, he slept with her only when, as he put it, the coast was clear. Everyone knew they were partners, so it was only natural they got together now and then, but he was scrupulously careful to see that it was not too often or mostly with other people, making them part of a group and not a definite twosome. As he said to Harriet: "Paula is quite capable of having me followed if she thought there was any danger of my seriously and quickly wanting my freedom. Better to let things proceed slowly so as not to arouse any suspicions, don't you agree?"

Harriet had agreed obediently, since she was already passionately in love with *Harriet Designs*, counting herself fortunate that Piers put appearances before pleasure. Now, she was conscious of a sense of unease. Piers was showing an uncharacteristic impatience, and she had enough on her plate, what with leaving her real true love to the anything but tender mercies of James Alexander.

He, she admitted, was the nail from which her own tenterhooks hung. The discreet enquiries she had made revealed an Everest of a reputation in their mutual field of expertise. Which should have relieved her mind but for some reason increased her edginess. She still felt he left a great deal to be desired, even if other women did not. On the contrary, they desired him. Evelyn was badly smitten while Miss Judd, a member of that endangered species: the implacable spinster, did not glower at him as she did at other men.

Why, then, did something about him raise her own every hackle in the alarm mode? What atavistic instinct was it that kept telling her he was trouble, and she was going to regret this? If only she did not have to take this holiday, but she was well aware that she was at the end of her physical tether. Discontent seemed to have set in and for the life of her she could not think why. She was an established success, she was financially secure, she had attained her every ambition. Why then, this nagging feeling of missing something. What? It was probably, she reasoned, her sense of anti-climax after what had been a long, hard climb. It had taken a lot of effort, after all, which was no doubt why she felt so tired. But she was at the top now, and the view was fantastic. Why then, did she feel so apprehensive, as though – as if – when she returned she would find her mountain had toppled into the valley below . . .

Piers insisted on accompanying her to Southampton, and once on board she found he had made her suite into a bower. With a brimming smile she turned to him, hugged him hard. Now that she was leaving him she found she did not want to. As if he too found the thought of six weeks (Harriet had absolutely refused to countenance even the thought of a three month absence and made it plain to all and sundry that it was six weeks or nothing) apart more than he could bear, he took her in his arms and proceeded to kiss her in a way that was totally unlike his usually restrained self.

24

"These have to last me a long time," he explained.

Harriet's dimples – one on either side of her mouth – appeared. "I shall console myself with thoughts of how pleased you will be on my return."

His arms tightened. "Then we really will celebrate; when you are your old self again, all bright and shining, full of your old vim and vigour, those shadows beneath your eyes erased . . ." he brushed them with his fingertips, "these beautiful bones covered with flesh." His hands at her waist almost met. "You are like a bird," he said fretfully, "so delicate and fragile . . ."

Harriet kissed him reassuringly. "You forget I have a stainless-steel structure."

"Miss me as much as I shall miss you?" he requested wistfully.

"What else will I have to think about?"

"The other Harriet."

"I have been warned off her. Mind you, I am relying on you to keep your eyes on what your friend James Alexander gets up to with her. In my opinion, his left hand not only has no idea what his right hand is up to, all his fingers act independently."

Piers gave her a sideways glance. "I keep telling you, James is absolutely trustworthy. Why do you suspect him of having ulterior motives?"

"Because he strikes me as a man with a full complement. It's not that I'm not grateful, I am, it's just that – well, why should a man like him consent to run a small, one-woman show, even if it is only for six weeks?"

"All you need worry about is that he *is* running it."

"But to come from a high-powered setup like Lewisohn's to my little shop in Brook Street is like flying a Tiger Moth after being captain of Concorde."

Piers turned away, shrugging. "Knowing James, he can probably do both."

"That's what I mean," said Harriet darkly.

The gong signalling All Visitors Ashore sounded. "No," Piers said quickly, as Harriet reached for her coat. "Don't come up on deck. It's cold and raining up there. Wait until you reach the sunshine then soak up as much as you can. Come back all toasted and golden – but send me postcards from every single port!"

"Promise," swore Harriet. In a sudden burst of affectionate gratitude she embraced him one last time. "Thank you so much for everything, not least for putting up with my bad temper and general crankiness over the last few months. I promise I will unwind. When I come back I will be all loose and pliable."

"That will be the day," Piers joked. They kissed one last time, then with a smile and a wave he was gone.

In spite of Piers' admonition Harriet did put on her coat and went up to watch the tugs taking the boat out. As he had said, it was a miserable day. She turned up her collar, but not until the ship was dropping its tugs did she return to her cabin. Well, she thought, as she did so, greater love hath no woman than she is willing to hand over her life's blood to a total stranger. I only hope your trust is not misplaced, my dear Piers . . .

Two

For the first few days out she was sorely tempted – almost driven – to call Piers and ask how things were going: only the thought of James Alexander's too-knowing smile imposed the curb. He had left her in no doubt as to his opinion of her mother-hen fixation with her alter ego. Which is ridiculous! she scorned. But it also made her bent and determined to show him that she *could* exist without it. And as the great white ship steamed southwards, incredulously she found herself unwinding, her uptightness dissolving, her doubts diminishing as her distance from them increased. By the end of her second week, she found she was actually grateful to her doctor for ordering her to come. She slept well and long, never less than ten hours a night. She rediscovered her appetite so as to be able to do justice to the good food served in the elegant restaurants. She sunbathed – with care for she burned easily – once they were into the Mediterranean, and at the end of the third week her white skin had been toasted to a golden apricot. She caught up on her reading, for Piers had stocked her room with two armfuls of novels, biographies, thrillers et al; she met people, dealt with a couple of predatory males who, though with wives, thought a lone woman was fair game even if the average age on board was at least twenty years her senior, and was invited to join the many day trips and excursions ashore, from where she dutifully sent the requisite postcards before going off to explore antique and curio shops, to examine silks and carpets and buy beautiful things, but judiciously and selectively so as not to need a pantechnicon when Piers turned up at Southampton to meet her. She was enjoying herself so much she began to find the days slipping by with alarming speed. It seemed like no time at all, never mind six whole weeks, before they were sailing back up Southampton Roads prepatory to docking. As she examined herself in the mirror before ringing for the steward to collect her luggage, she thought smugly. Well, Piers, I think I can say I will be able to meet every one of your specifications. I only hope to God that James Alexander has met mine . . .

But it was not Piers who came to find her when the ship docked. It was her 'locum', almost hidden behind an over-the-top sheaf of blood-red roses. In the face of Harriet's surprise he said plaintively: "The least you can do is say hello."

"You were the last person I expected," she told him truthfully, annoyed to be caught on the hop.

"But the first to say 'welcome back'." His eyes went over her in a way as to make her intensely aware of them. "No need to ask if the rest has done you good. You *are* Harriet Hilliard? Not some Hollywood movie star—"

"You can put your flannel away," Harriet told him crisply. "I washed my hands and face before I came."

He laughed, and thrusting the roses at her bent to kiss her unprepared mouth. "From Piers," he said blandly, "the kiss and the roses. You see before you a poor substitute. At the last minute he had to meet some very important Arabs, so he deputised me. All I have to do is carry out his explicit instructions, and the first one is to put your mind at rest about the shop, where all is is well; in the pink, in fact, even if that is not your colour. Not that you look particularly worried, I am glad to see. The shadows beneath those remarkable eyes have packed their bags and gone, while the rest of you has – shall we say filled out? – and to a remarkable degree."

"I have regained every pound I lost," Harriet told him pointedly.

"It shows. In all the right places. Obviously your six week separation from your lifeline was not as unbearable as you thought."

Harriet turned away, ostensibly to pick up her coat, in reality annoyed that he not only should see so much but have the temerity to say so. Then: with those eyes? she asked herself derisively. But she determined not to let him rile her.

"If you give me your baggage checks I'll see to everything. I have my car," he offered.

It was a beautiful Jaguar XJS, the colour of the roses. He had her through customs in no time, bags in the boot or on the back seat, after having arranged for the despatch of her booty in a way that denoted a very experienced traveller, pausing only to say: "I see you did not entirely forget the other Harriet, then. This little lot looks like the contents of every shop between here and Istanbul."

"Just a few things I could not resist."

"Then they must be quite something. I had you down as a lady possessed of the ultimate in sales resistance."

29

Harriet opened her mouth to blast him then changed her mind. Rising to his bait only made him cast it further.

When finally they drove off he said: "Right, now you can cross-examine me as to the happenings of the last six weeks."

"I have no intention of doing any such thing," Harried replied untruthfully.

"Of course you have," he returned unfazed. "I've been on trial, after all."

"My name is Hilliard, not Jeffreys."

"Oh, I have no doubts as to my acquittal – once you have weighed the evidence, of course."

"No problems? Not even with Mrs Harcourt-Smith? How did you find her?"

"Everywhere I turned. But the penthouse is done and she's happy. So much so she plans a house-warming next week to which you are cordially invited. That way you get to mark my essay on early Goldwyn-girl, but I warn you, I expect at least an A-plus."

"No trailing draperies? No coloured glass figurines?"

"Nary a one. All is pure Harriet Hilliard, and we all know how pure *she* is." Harriet glanced at him swiftly but his face was as bland as his voice. "I did give in once or twice just so as to let her feel she was having her own way."

"And everything else?"

He gave her a succinct rundown. If it was true – and it will be, she thought with something like chagrin, it will be – then she had nothing to worry about.

"You will find my written report on your desk. I thought you would like it all in black and white; one of my favourite colour combinations until I saw what blue and yellow can do."

Their eyes met in the mirror and as they locked glances Harriet found herself unaccountably flushing. So she asked quickly: "How did you keep Mrs Harcourt-Smith away from her sweet-pea sicklies?"

"I side-tracked her. The power of suggestion is worth a dozen power struggles. That is why the two of you collided, woman to woman. I, on the other hand, am a man."

"You don't say," marvelled Harriet, and now it was his turn to flash her a quick glance followed by a grin.

Slowing down for a curve he took it then changed gear before accelerating away down the straight. he was a very good driver; without seeming to exert any effort, he anticipated, foresaw, and took the necessary action, rarely having to brake, slow or avoid. He had the reflexes of one of the great cats.

"Sadie" (*Sadie*! thought Harriet) "is the product of her generation," he went on. "The kind that coerced women into believing they were useless without a man to lean on, and that the kind who didn't – or wouldn't – such as your ever efficient Miss Judd, ended up as grim-faced spinsters, except that Miss Judd is anything but. All I had to do was let Sadie lean because all she really wanted was someone to listen to her and make all the right noises."

"And what were they?"

"Ah, if I divulge my methods I might not have the same success rate."

"Sadie Harcourt-Smith never struck me as a lady who did not know exactly what she wanted at any given time," Harriet said caustically.

31

"Oh, she does. Where you went wrong was in insisting she have what you want."

"What do you mean, went wrong?" Harriet vaulted onto her high horse.

"I mean you argued. She told me. Yet all the time she was always open to persuasion."

"So you persuaded her?"

"Like I said, she is of the generation that thinks women should always heed a man."

"What on earth for?"

"Because, unlike you, she is neither independent nor self-sufficient. You would consider relying on a man – on anyone – to be sign of weakness on your part. Sadie's way forward was to rely on a whole succession of men, all of them willing to supply the necessary wherewithal in return for that reliance."

"You mean she sold herself." Harriet's voice curled at the edges with distaste.

Again she was aware of his glance but he said mildly, "I told you. Different generations. She was a stunning woman in her youth – I've seen the photographs – but all she had was her beauty. Even if she had been gifted with your drive and determination, not to mention your brains, she would still have been hard put to apply them. Thirty-five years ago women were deflected and discouraged from doing so. With your generation it is different."

"Thank God! When I went to Piers I was selling my abilities only."

"Yet you ended up with him."

"Not because of any intent on my part. He was—" For some reason she could not hit on the right word but he did:

"A bonus?"

"Yes, that's it exactly. All I wanted was financial backing."

"A lot of women would have taken both."

Chin tilted: "I am not most women. The fact that Piers is a rich man is not my reason for agreeing to marry him."

"I am perfectly well aware of that, and while we are on the subject, I think you will find that he has some news for you in that direction."

"Oh?" Harriet's *frisson* was as instinctive as her frown until she caught sight of it in the mirror and smoothed it away hastily.

"He is absolutely dying to tell you."

Harriet opened her mouth to ask: "Since you are his deputy why don't you?" then closed it again. Instinct warned her it would not do to get involved with this man in a discussion as to the struggle Piers was having to free himself from his erring wife. "No doubt," she contented herself with saying.

"He is like a dog with two tails," James went on, before taking her breath away by following up with a swift: "Why aren't you?"

"I don't yct know what it is, do I?" she came back.

James clicked his tongue in a way that had Harriet grinding her teeth. "Come now, Harriet. Isn't it obvious?"

"One cannot always tell, even from the obvious."

"Then why don't you hazard a guess?"

"I prefer fact to fiction."

James sighed. "Yes, of course you do, don't you?" Sorrowfully: "Is there no romance in your soul, Harriet? You independent ladies are taking away all the imagination and dreams from the battle between the sexes."

That did it. "In the first place," Harriet bit off her words in chunks, "I am not one of your 'ladies', and in the second I am not involved in any battle."

"Which makes me wonder why."

Harriet ignored that. "To be independent – in your terminology – one has first of all to have been dependant. I never have."

"I know. Piers told me you have always done your own thing."

"I have no need for labels or banners, Mr Alexander. I have always been and ever will be only my own mistress."

That silenced him, she thought smugly, for they drove on in silence until he turned into a pleasant-looking hotel as they approached Guildford.

"Piers will be tied up all day so there is no need to hurry," he explained blithely, and over lunch kept the conversation general. Even so, they found themselves ranged on opposite sides on more than one issue. As they sparred, but good-naturedly now, Harriet put away a large lunch, and afterwards they sat talking over coffee, or rather James talked and Harriet listened. He had lived in six countries before he was sixteen – his father had been a high-ranking diplomat with the United Nations; it was while he was at a conference in San Fransisco that he had met James' mother, who was a native of that city. James was the third of their four children; he had two older sisters and a younger brother. Now that his father was retired, his parents spent half the year in London and the rest of it in California.

When at last he looked at his watch to say regretfully: "I think we had better be on our way," Harriet was astonished to find it was after half-past three. The rest of the journey went quickly, for they kept away from contentious subjects, and when the Jaguar drew up outside her house in Pont Street it was to find Piers' Bentley already on a meter.

"Told you," James commented. "He's probably hopping from foot to foot. You will invite me to the wedding, won't you?"

"Well, you were at his other one, weren't you?" Harriet observed sweetly.

"Piers told you, I see."

"That you introduced him to Paula? Yes."

"My motives were entirely selfish at the time, but in all fairness I did warn him. Piers may be a financial genius but what he knows about women you could inscribe on the head of a pin." He got out of the car to open first Harriet's door then that of the rear and the boot, so he could get at her bags. "I won't come up," he said. "You open the front door and I'll put this lot in the hall Piers can carry them up later." He carried the bags up the front steps and left them in the hall.

"Thank you," Harriet said, "for everything, I mean. Especially the last six weeks I will admit I was not entirely sold on the idea at first—"

"You don't say?" he observed dryly.

"I only went along with it for Piers' sake, but from what you have told me it seems he was right. Mind you – " her dimples appeared, " – I have yet to see what you have done for Mrs Harcourt-Smith."

"I followed your specification to the letter."

"I can't wait to see it."

"You will have to; the house-warming is a week away."

35

"Will you be in the shop on Monday?"

"Yes; to hand over all official-like."

As Harriet turned to go. "May I say it has been a pleasure," he said, "not to mention an education . . ."

Piers was rapturous at her appearance. "Darling, my love . . . you look fabulous! A tan suits you no end and you have put back all that lost weight. I can feel it! It becomes you no end. Once more you are a curvaceous armful. I was right, wasn't I? You have profited from your R&R?"

"Yes, you were right to insist that I went. Thank you for doing so." She hugged and kissed him.

"And James has managed splendidly, just like I knew he would. He's got that Harcourt-Smith woman hanging on his every word, the shop is running on oiled wheels and he was awfully good about collecting you. I really couldn't make it, darling. I had this frightfully important meeting. You didn't mind?" He looked anxious, remembering her dislike of his friend.

"No," Harriet answered truthfully.

"Good, now come and sit down. I want to know everything . . . where did you go and who did you meet and what was it like . . .?"

Harriet allowed herself to be drawn down to give him a blow-by-blow account, he interrupting her now and again to kiss and caress her as if he could not keep his hands off her. He confessed as much. "You look so much better, dearest. I can't get over the difference in you. All rested and your sparkle back. And I've got some news that will make you sparkle even more brightly. Paula has agreed to institute immediate divorce proceedings on the grounds of the irrevocable breakdown of the marriage!" Triumphantly: "What do you think of that, then?"

Prepared as she had been by James Alexander, Harriet did not so much think as feel – as though someone had slammed a fist in her stomach.

"I knew you would be surprised," Piers said happily.

"But – what caused this sudden change of heart?"

"Believe it or not – it was James."

I knew it! Harriet thought in a searing flash of rage, her previously charitable feelings vapouring in the heat. That devious bastard! I was right. He did have an ulterior motive!

"I happened to mention what you had said about her finding a substitute and damn me if James didn't go and introduce her to some American Croesus – an acquaintance of his mother."

"An amazing man, your friend James," Harriet observed from between clenched teeth.

Totally caught up in his joy, Piers missed the serrated edge to her voice. "Isn't he though? I told you he knows absolutely everybody."

Before she could stop them the words exploded from Harriet's mouth. "What does he get? A commission?" She consigned Mr James Alexander to hell. How dare he do this? Mr Interference himself. The cheek of the man! The infernal, brass-bound nerve of him!

"Oh, now Harriet . . . We ought to be grateful. He was only trying to help . . ."

Yes, himself, Harriet thought rancorously. He is playing some deeper game here. I had that feeling about him from the start. Is it any wonder I didn't trust him? What is he really after . . .

She chewed on it all weekend, during which she

fought her way through a thicket of unpleasant facts, every one of them leaving deep and painful scratches on her peace of mind. The one that bled most was the thought of Paula Cayzer freeing her husband to marry one Harriet Hilliard. It also stung with painful dismay. There was no way, she realised with a deep sense of shock-horror, that she wished to become The Hon. Mrs Piers Cayzer. She had never expected to have to do so and had only said yes because she believed the likelihood was as far removed as Mars. What she had done, she realised as she recoiled from the body she had just tripped over, was cold-bloodedly use Piers as a smokescreen behind which she could devote all her time and attention to what really mattered: *Harriet Designs*. He had given her not only financial independence, he had provided a masculine presence in her life, affording her at the same time both protection and emotional freedom from other men. Stricken, she gazed at the hideous fact that while she had worked like a beaver to repay her financial debt to him, she had never so much as given a thought to the emotional one.

Oh, my God, she moaned, falling into a chair, staring at the ugly truth which was likewise staring her out of countenance: what *have* I done? She did not love Piers; she liked him, she was fond of him in an almost motherly way, but the prospect of spending the rest of her life with him was not a pleasing one. In fact, it made her draw the curtains.

The trouble was she had promised she would, and on the strength of that promise he had waited and hoped for years now; protecting her, standing by her. Which was when she realised something else. It was precisely because Piers was a nineteen nineties man with eighteen nineties ethics that she had picked him.

She was so distraught she took to pacing the carpet in her agitation. That she, Harriet Hilliard, always so scrupulously honest – and that was because she wanted no strings in her dealings with people – should turn out to be as emotionally dishonest as they came left her feeling as if she had just been thrust, stark naked, into a roomful of strangers. She wanted to die of shame. And then, as it tended to do these days, her mood swung as rage flooded her. It was all Mr James bloody Alexander's fault. Him and his unwanted interference. Damn him! she seethed, beating her fist on the mantelpiece. Damn him to hell and back! I *knew* he was trouble the moment I set eyes on him. What am I going to do? In God's name what am I going to do!

Staring into the highly polished shield she had awarded herself for Effort and Achievement, she seemed to see behind her reflection the malevolent grin of her own personal demon. It seemed to be taunting: 'Don't ask me. You got yourself into this situation; now get yourself out'. She had expected to come back from her cruise to pick up the perfectly aligned threads (neatly sorted, of course, into colour and fabric) of her well-ordered life exactly as she had left them, only to find that James Alexander had emptied every drawer and strewn those threads all over the place, leaving a tangle she had no idea how to begin to unravel.

Why, oh why, she berated herself, did you say anything to Piers about finding Paula a substitute?

'Because you were convinced it was the last thing that could or would happen', her personal demon answered. And it wouldn't, if he had been on his own, but since his old friend James Alexander came on the scene Piers has taken to doing lots of things that you would never have expected of him.

"Old Friend!" Harriet spat viciously. "Interfering Nosy Parker more-like." But she could not take her eyes from the Final Demand lying on her mat, knowing with a sick, hollow feeling inside that one way or another, she had to to find the wherewithal to pay it.

Three

S he went warily into the office on Monday morning determined, now that she knew what James Alexander was capable of, to stay at Red Alert. She was still not absolutely certain as to what game he was playing, only that it was a devious one, and that she and Piers were pawns in it.

But he was affability's self. Not by so much as a raised eyebrow did he betray the slightest interest in what he damned well had to know was occupying her mind to the exclusion of everything else. Oh, he was clever, she fretted furiously. There was no way she could take him to task since that would show her hand; all she could do was wait and see what he would do next, and the first thing he did was tell her that Sadie Harcourt-Smith wanted him to go over some small final details with her before the house-warming, so he would be around for the time being – if that was all right with Harriet, of course.

If it was all right! As if she had a choice! Now he had the perfect excuse to hang about and meddle some more, and if he didn't deliberately arrange it that way then I don't know Biedermayer from Buhl! she thought. Now what has he got up that three-button sleeve? Which was why, once behind her desk in her office, she went through everything with her fine-tooth comb. Not that she needed to, since Miss Judd and Evelyn sang nothing but peals of praise until Harriet wished she was tone deaf. That afternoon the man himself gave her a detailed rundown on what was what as far as he was concerned, interrupted twice by telephone calls from Mrs Harcourt-Smith, whom he called Sadie in such a way as to have her arch giggle echoing from the receiver. Harriet kept her mouth tight shut, ever mindful of the fat fee she was making from this particular commission, plus the fact that it was none of her business how he handled clients as long as they were happy. And obviously Sadie Harcourt-Smith was not so much happy as delirious.

Her own mood took a further turn for the worse when, on resuming their discussions, she discovered that the manufacturer she had failed to persuade to supply her a special kind of slubbed silk in weeks rather than months, had now agreed to let Mr Alexander have it in a fortnight. He was competition, all right, and since competition had always dug in its spurs where Harriet was concerned, she determined not only to meet it but beat it.

For the rest of that final week before the housewarming she woke up every morning raring to go, eager for combat in the hand-to-hand – or rather tongue-to-tongue where her rival was concerned – battle in which she was engaged. He only had to let fall the slightest hint of criticism and she would pore over a design, searching for the flaw – usually to find there was one, such as the fact that when he had suggested a Chippendale rather than a Louis XVI cabinet in the drawing room of the house she was doing in The Boltons, he was dead right. And when she

42

was trying to explain to the man who mixed her paints the exact shade of seawater-green she wanted for the Docklands penthouse she had designed, James took up a brush from her drawing table and proceeded to mix blue and yellow to produce the exact – the absolutely perfect – shade.

He was also an expert on furniture, paintings and porcelain. "Sotheby's is the perfect training ground," he answered, when she asked with sardonic irritation where he had acquired his store of knowledge, but he was a godsend when it came to spotting a fake. He saved Harriet a small fortune when the chairs she believed, as the dealer swore, to be genuine Hepplewhite, turned out to be twentieth century facsimiles.

"Always look at the joints," he advised. "They should have been fitted by hand because they did not have the technology to do anything else back then. This chair has been turned on a machine . . . very skilfully, but even so . . . Look at the edges there." He handed her a magnifying glass and sure enough, there were the tell-tale traces.

He handled porcelain and crystal with both care and long-fingered dexterity. The same way he handled people. Miss Judd's suffragette severity melted at his very appearance on the scene, while Evelyn took every opportunity to consult him on this or that. Even Harriet found herself revelling in their daily confrontations to the extent that, incredible though it was, the thought of Piers, Paula and the impending divorce were thrust to the back of her mind. Instead, she found herself pondering every morning on what to wear, because on one of them, when he had eyed her dark red Donna Karan suit, he had shaken his head and said:

"Not your colour, Harriet." When she got home that night, after taking it off she told Annie, her house-keeper, that she could take it to the Nearly New shop.

"It does my heart good to see you back on top form," Piers told her enthusiastically. "That cruise worked marvels."

But Harriet knew it was not the cruise. It was competition. That had ever put the spur to her abilities; never failed to give her the charge she needed. James Alexander was stimulation and then some. Which was when she realised something else: that was what she had been missing for so long.

She went to the Harcourt-Smith housewarming with keen anticipation, eager to see just how James had managed to restrain that lady's wilder flights of fancy, for she had firmly refused to let Harriet take up those particular reins again.

"James knows exactly what I want," she told Harriet in her iron-butterfly way. "He seems to be able to read my mind."

Not surprising since there is only one thing on it, Harriet thought, before saying politely: "I am only too happy to allow Mr Alexander to continue to fulfil your requirements."

"Oh, he does, Miss Hilliard, he most certainly does."

James escorted Harriet to Eton Square. Piers never went to any of Harriet's housewarmings. Mr Circum-spection himself, he pointed out that while to the world at large he was her sleeping partner, it would not do to let people know that he occupied the position literally as well as metaphorically.

James called for her promptly at eight, and black tie suited him no end, serving somehow to emphasise his total masculinity. He, in turn, admired her, saying approvingly: "It may have taken time and effort, my dear Harriet, but I assure you the result is well worth it. Now that *is* your colour; it matches your eyes."

Of matt silk crepe, the dress – by her favourite designer Jean Muir – was both cunningly and superbly cut, narrowly fitted in all the right places yet soft and fluid and flowing to the body, gleaming dully in the light.

"I am so relieved," she said, with an edge to her voice on which he could have shaved. "Now I can relax and enjoy myself."

"I trust you will. Yours is, after all, the ultimate accolade."

"What are you expecting – Victor Ludorum?"

"Oh, I got that at school, but certainly a high pass mark."

Their hostess must have been watching for them – or rather him – because she pounced as soon as they arrived, her face lighting at the sight of James in a way that stunned Harriet. Why you cold-blooded devil! she thought appalled. So that was how you "handled" her! You have got her hooked, gaffed and in the basket! It outraged her. That was NOT what she had told him to do.

"James . . . and Miss Hilliard." For Harriet her smile was only sixty-watt. "How nice to see you looking so well, but as your absence was responsible for bringing me James then I am doubly pleased. You must have been inspired."

Yes, but not by what you think, Harriet told her silently.

"Now, do go and look for yourself," Sadie Harcourt-Smith waved a heavily jewelled hand in the direction of the madding throng. "I want to introduce James to some important people."

Harriet's eyes narrowed as she said; "Setting up on your own?" to him.

"Right now, I am giving my all to *Harriet Designs*, as you will see when you do your tour of inspection. Your instructions have been carried out to the letter."

"Just so long as the signature is mine."

"Forgery is something *I* do not go in for," he replied, in such a way as to make her stiffen, but Sadie Harcourt-Smith was leading him away.

"Do help yourself to champagne," she said over her shoulder.

Fixing a smile and nodding at those faces she knew, those same faces which turned up at every house-warming, Harriet set off to give the penthouse the third degree.

All was as she had designed it. He had curbed Sally's tendency to excess and restrained her vulgarity. Only now and again could Harriet see where that lady had dug in her pedicured toes. She and Harriet had fought ten rounds concerning Sadie's desire for a bed shaped like a swan, draped in shell-pink chiffon, and while James had cleverly let her have her way as to colour, it was not the dainty little-finger-raised-pink she wanted but silvery and muted, both subtle and sophisticated, nor was it chiffon, it was slubbed silk. And the bed was no swan. It was a superb example of Napoleonic opulence; at once rich yet plain, dominating the room from its centre, where James had placed it.

Now where did he find *that*, Harriet thought on a pang of pure envy. He must know something – no, some*one* as it was him – she didn't, because in her searches through the dealers and warehouses she had not come across anything so sumptuous. She was standing behind it, obscured from view as she examined the way the silk was gathered into a crown from which it fell in superb folds to the velvet pile of the carpet, when she heard a triumphantly vindictive voice exclaim:

"There now – what did I tell you? Did you ever see such a bed? It once belonged to Pauline Bonaparte."

A second female voice giggled. "Do you think Sadie is trying a little emulation on for size?"

"As if she has a chance! She's got twenty years on him. Besides, Rina is currently *maîtresse en titre*."

"Do you suppose Sadie knows?"

"About Rina? Darling, Rina has long made sure that everybody does."

"She isn't here tonight."

"No, he brought Sadie's interior designer with him – Harriet Hilliard? The one who did all this little extravaganza. You know James stood in for her while she went on a six week cruise. Overwork, they said. Sheer frustration if you ask me."

"Frustration? Why?"

"She is the one Piers Cayzer is trying to ditch Paula for."

"No! Are you sure? I haven't heard a word."

"Oh, it's very much under wraps, but I have it on the *very* best authority."

"Well, I suppose she is at the other end of the spectrum from Paula, who is not one of my favourite people. I heard she has her milksop husband in a half nelson and there is no way he can free himself."

"Oh, it's been years now, and she won't let such a prize go without a knock-out, drag-down fight. She is the last woman to take account of birds in the bushes – even if that is where she spends so much of her time. No wonder that Hilliard woman had a nervous breakdown. I mean, so near and yet so far . . . All that lovely money held fast in Paula's tightly clenched hands."

"Just as well Sadie has plenty. She'll need something with which to entice James Alexander. The queue stretches from here to eternity."

"Well, you did try to jump it, darling."

"Only when you gave up your place, sweetie."

Harriet could all but see the knives flashing.

"Let's face it. Rina has him right now and God help anyone who tries to dislodge her."

"So why is he here with the hired help?"

"Strictly business. Piers Cayzer and his millions are her quarry."

"But she must earn a bomb doing up places like this."

"True, but still chicken-feed compared to a man who owns his very own merchant bank . . ." There were more giggles then the voices faded.

Harriet found she was clutching the silk hangings so tightly her knuckles were white. As she released her grip she saw with a detached part of her mind that the material had not creased. Well done, she thought automatically, for the rest of her was struggling to deal with the fact that it was absolutely true what they said about eavesdroppers. Those vicious harpies, she thought disbelievingly. *Me* a gold-digger!!! I have paid back every penny I ever borrowed from Piers. And he left Paula long before he made any moves in my direction, never mind asked me to marry him. So much for your scrupulous avoidance of gossip, my dear Piers. It is an open secret that you and I are a pair, even if the reasons why are wrong.

She felt besmirched, even though she knew of the coterie and their ever-wagging tongues: the set that attended all the housewarmings for one reason only: to look for dirt in the shape of the latest *on dits*; to dissect people and disseminate gossip. Like James Alexander and this Rina, whoever she was. To find out that she was part of their nasty speculations made her feel distaste to the point of wanting to reach for the mouthwash. Her first instinct was to storm after those two bitches and give them a tongue-lashing, but that would only serve to pour fat on the fire, and the last thing needed in this hideously expensive house was a conflagration. But the more she thought about it the more anger she felt. In no way was she the woman those two had shredded. All I ever wanted from Piers was financial backing, she thought indignantly. And that has been repaid.

'Yes, in coin', her demon reminded slyly.

She was standing there, rooted with shock and anger, when she heard other voices approaching the bedroom, so she slipped into the adjoining bathroom. It was large and sybaritic, with the sunken bath Sadie had wanted, and the chaise-longue just like the one she had once seen in some technicolour extravaganza, but again, while James had let her have her way as to the things she wanted – Harriet had tried to talk her out of both – he had reined her in as to their design and

49

colour. Locking the door, Harriet sat down and set about restoring her self-esteem.

So her six week absence had been due to teeth-gnashing impatience at the delay in becoming the second Mrs Piers Cayzer, had it? The hell it had! Harriet was no prude, but the thought that the *mondaine* had her labelled and classified mortified her, put her in the same class as that Rina woman they had mentioned. What was it they had called her? *Maîtresse en titre*. Damned cheek! How dare they put her and Piers into that category. He, of course, would be appalled, not that she intended to tell him. The less he knew the better.

She felt she was being got at. All of a sudden her tranquil, well-ordered life was shaking, and she placed the responsibility squarely at the well-shod feet of James Alexander. He was the catalyst all right. It was since his appearance on the scene that everything had begun to fall apart. Why, oh *why* had Piers brought him on stage? Him and his cold-blooded manipulation of Sadie Harcourt-Smith, not to mention his unforgivable interference in her own, very private life. Let him mind his own business, such as this Rina person. The name rang a bell in her memory. It was familiar yet she could not put a face to it . . . Yes! Of course! That was what they called her. The Face. Rina Cunningham, the Supermodel. The original Playmate of the Western World, even if she had not yet displayed herself nude as the centrefold. Her body was as famous as her face. No wonder those two bitches had felt sorry for Sadie Harcourt-Smith. She had not a hope in hell against Rina Cunningham. No ordinary woman did.

Harriet visualised the picture that had graced the cover of Vogue a month or two back. Rina adrift in a Versace fantasy of layered organza ranging from deepest flamingo-pink to palest cloud-grey, her autumn leaf hair aflame above her glorious emerald eyes; matchless cabochons of depth and fire, gazing out from a face of such beauty it took the breath away. So that was where his taste lay. Poor Sadie . . . The thought of being on the hook of a man like James Alexander was one which made Harriet shudder.

At that moment she heard his voice through the door, ". . . seen Harriet, have you? I can't seem to find her . . ."

No, and you won't either, Harriet thought. She gave it five more minutes then went in search of her hostess, found her the centre of an admiring crowd of which he, thank God, was not part, a fact which Sadie obviously regretted since her smile was wan as Harriet said: "I have seen enough to know that I need not have worried. Everything is absolutely perfect."

"Isn't it, though? He is the most marvellous m – decorator – as are you, of course," was tacked on hastily.

"As long as you are satisfied."

"Oh, the house is perfect . . . James is an asset to your firm, Miss Hilliard. I would keep him under lock and key if I were you."

Where he's got you? thought Harriet. Not on your life. Shaking hands once more she went to fetch her black velvet coat, but coming out into the hall again she found Sadie's one unfulfilled desire waiting for her.

"There you are! I have been reduced to looking under beds."

51

"Better than having to look in them," Harriet riposted. "I am off now. I have seen what I came for. No need to drag yourself away. I can get a cab – oh," she turned to face him, "– and full marks, by the way. Alpha Plus, I think."

She saw the inky eyes gleam but before he could come back an opulent brunette inserted herself between them. "James, darling, you are not leaving! The night is young."

Which is more than I can say for you, Harriet thought, recognising the voice as belonging to one of the harpies.

"Do let's have a chat . . . I haven't seen you in an age . . ."

But James removed the talon tipped hand which had fastened on his forearm. "Sorry," he said pleasantly, "but I was taught always to leave with the lady I came with."

The brunette turned to survey Harriet with insolent eyes. "Since when have you kept such early hours, James?"

"I always do when I am working."

The way the eyes flickered meant the tongue was about to, Harriet surmised, and was proved right when the brunette drawled: "Is that what you call it?"

"I do, because that is exactly what it is." James' tone of voice had her hand snaking back at the double.

"Don't let me keep you, then." Nastily she added, "Rina will never believe it."

"Rina never believes anything unless she sees it for herself," he told her cheerfully. "Ready, Harriet?"

As they went down in the lift: "She was right, you

52

know, it is early," James said. "Would you like to go on somewhere?"

"No, thank you."

"Ah, yes, Piers will be ringing you at half-past ten as usual."

Is there anything he hasn't told you? Harriet thought balefully.

They were in his car when he asked: "Might I enquire as to the state of play in the war Piers and Paula are fighting?"

"Since you were instrumental in opening up the Second Front I should have thought your intelligence reports would be bang up to date."

"Do I detect a note of disapproval?"

"I prefer to be consulted about matters that concern me."

"Ah . . . in other words, I should leave Piers to fight his own battles."

"I was not aware there had been a call for general mobilisation."

He threw back his head and laughed. "Harriet, you are a girl after my own heart. If you were a real Designing Woman and pitted one tenth of the wit, strength and brains you used to create *Harriet Designs* against your enemy in this particular battle it would have been your victory a long time ago."

"Piers and I agreed that I should keep well out of it. Paula Cayzer is no concern of mine."

She could have bitten out her tongue when he chided: "But she should be, Harriet. She most certainly should be." Thoughtfully. "You know, for a strong-minded lady who has flattened her own mountain, this is one Rock of Gibraltar you are prepared to let Piers tunnel through with a teaspoon. Such monumental patience is quite out of your character: does not match up with the rest of you."

"What you think is of no importance, and I do not see why my affairs should be any concern of yours."

"Affairs, Harriet?"

Goaded: "You know damn well what I mean. Just acknowledge that my business is none of your business."

"Oh, I have already acknowledged certain very salient facts about you, not least of which is that you are not – anything but, in fact – what Piers thinks you are." For once in her life Harriet was at a loss for words because he had taken her breath away. "In fact," James continued, "you are a fraud."

Harriet had turned into a stalagmite. How on earth had he discovered so quickly what she had only just discovered for herself? Luckily the car was slowing prepatory to stopping at her front door so she groped for the door handle, conscious of a stong desire to run. But the handle did not move.

"Locks from the dash," James said laconically. "With my reputation would you expect anything else?"

Harriet found her voice. "I expect nothing from you."

"I know. That is what intrigues me."

"Kindly open the door."

"In a minute." She heard him sigh. "You disappoint me, Harriet. And for the first time. I remember you telling me that you preferred fact to fiction and now, here you are believing your own fairy story." Another sigh, sounding mournful. "Ah, well, perhaps it is too soon . . ."

There was a click and the door gave. Harriet all but fell out before he could come round and open it. Escape was her one thought, but she managed to snarl: "Where you are concerned it is already far too late."

She did not bid him good-night; the way she slammed his car door expressed her feelings perfectly, so did her stiff back as she stalked up the steps to her front door where she managed, with a badly shaking hand, to insert her key and open it, but once it closed behind her she leaned back against it, legs turned to jelly and in a state of frantic disbelief. How had he seen? When had she given herself away? Frantically searching her memory she could find no time or place, no self-revealing words that would have told him to look behind her façade for what he had so obviously discovered concealed behind it. And it could not possibly be Piers either, because he had not the slightest inkling. Then how . . . HOW on earth had James Alexander come to understand – and with such perceptive certainty – that marrying Piers was the last thing she wanted; that she was indeed a fraud. What had led him so quickly to that conclusion when she had only just realised it for herself?

He was even more dangerous than she thought. Thank God he was about to go his own way, since the sooner he was out of her life the better if she was to retain any control of it.

55

Four

T hat night – or rather early next morning – Harriet went home.

By the time Piers rang, on the dot of half-past ten as usual, she had her planned story pat, which was that she was going into the country next day to see a prospective client. A contact made at the housewarming, she said, and one that necessitated striking while the iron was at maximum heat. He accepted her story without question, as she knew he would. She had lied to Piers only once; at the very beginning of their relationship when he had enquired about her background. She had told him her parents were dead and that she was alone in the world. He therefore had no idea she had any home other than her flat in Pont Street or that the one she was fleeing to now – with no coherent reason except the urge to get as far away as possible – was the one where she had been born and her mother had, until recent months, lived alone.

By six a.m. she was in her steel blue Volvo Turbo Estate – useful for fabric samples, the odd piece of furniture, lamps, pictures and so on, driving North on the M1. It was only a couple of hours drive and she had not long been on her way when it began to rain, in keeping with her mood; teetering on the edge of a precipice, knowing that what she was afraid of was coming up fast behind her and that she either had to jump or turn and make a stand. Her instinct was to go to ground, and the only place she could think of was the house she had left at eighteen to go to Goldsmiths College.

It was just gone eight when she turned into the small, tree-lined cul-de-sac of redbrick, three-bedroom, pre-war semis, all of them quiet, behind still drawn curtains, especially her mother's house. Empty now. Her father was dead and for the past three months her mother had been in a nursing home for chronic alcoholics.

When she opened the front door, stepped into the narrow hall, smelled the old familiar smell of polish and the mustiness of a house kept closed, she was conscious of an overwhelming relief. She was safe here, since nobody she knew had any idea it existed.

Hit by a sudden wave of tiredness, for she had not slept a wink, she went straight upstairs to what had been her bedroom, overlooking the back garden. It was exactly the way it had been when she had left it for the last time. Her mother had changed nothing. Falling onto her bed she closed her eyes and almost at once was asleep.

A car horn awoke her, and looking at her watch she saw it was two o'clock. She felt calmer now that she was rested, her frantic sense of urgency gone. She sat up, saw that her suit was all creased, but instead of getting up to take it off lay back and looked around the little room where she had slept for the first eighteen years of her life.

It had sprigged wallpaper, with matching curtains

and bedcover. "Matching curtains!" her mother had sniffed. "They will make the room awfully monotonous. Far better a plain cotton in one of the colours – and why painted furniture – white at that!" In Mrs Hilliard's opinion, good solid mahogany or walnut was far more sensible. But Harriet had bought whitewood which she glossed herself, afterwards stencilling it in her favourite Wedgewood blue, and she made the curtains and bedcover herself on her mother's old treadle Singer. She lay and gazed up at the ceiling – stencilled to match the furniture, at which her mother had pursed her lips, but as Harriet had been paying from the proceeds of her Saturday job at Marks and Spencers, she had not been able to carry the day – and thought she should telephone the Home; see if it was convenient to see her mother. Leaving the bed she went along to the bathroom, where she switched on the immersion heater before going for her briefcase to get her mobile phone. On enquiring if her mother was up to receiving visitors she was told she was, and that four o'clock would be fine. That done, she went back upstairs, took off her suit and hung it behind the bathroom door so that the steam from her bath would erase the creases, before putting on an old robe – her mother had never parted with the clothes Harriet left behind – and going down to the kitchen where she filled the electric kettle, feeling the need for a restorative cup of tea. While it was boiling she found an unopened packet of crispbreads in the cupboard and took some low-fat spread from the freezer. There was also marmalade in the cupboard and a stock of long-life milk, kept for those occasions when she came to visit her mother. She made tea, then sitting at the kitchen table ate a couple of buttered Ryvita with marmalade, accompanying them with two cups of tea, meanwhile leafing through such mail as there was, mostly circulars and advertising bumph. Utility bills were sent on to her by her mother's neighbour, Mrs McBride, who also kept an eye on the house.

By the time she had washed her mug and plate, the water was hot enough for her to rinse out her bra, pants and tights, which she hung in the airing cupboard to dry. While her bath was running she poured in a hefty dollop of the Floris Lily of the Valley bubbling bath oil she had bought her mother one Christmas, for some reason still on the side of the bath, no doubt not taken to the nursing home because her mother had said, as she so often had: "Lifebuoy soap has always been perfectly good enough for me, thank you".

She was ready to go at three-thirty, but her destination was only a twenty minute drive away, so she stopped on the way to buy a sheaf of mixed flowers and a box of her mother's favourite Turkish delight – she had a sweet tooth – along with an armful of magazines.

The nursing home, once the country estate of a wealthy industrialist, was set in spacious and well-kept grounds, with a lake and formal gardens. Mrs Hilliard had a ground-floor room at the back overlooking the lawns, with a pretty view. It was comfortably furnished and the staff were pleasant and highly trained. The fees reflected the care but then, Harriet thought sardonically, she could well afford them. The nurse on duty at the reception desk recognised her and greeted her pleasantly.

"How is my mother?" Harriet asked.

"Oh, up and down, you know . . . I'm afraid we have to watch her constantly these days though, because she has the most amazing facility for getting hold of the hard stuff. We don't allow her spending money any more, by the way. She was bribing people to bring bottles in. So please, Miss Hilliard, if you wish to leave money for her, hand it in at the office and they will give you a receipt. She'll be glad of the chocolates, though. She does dote on them. Do you mind waiting a few minutes? Doctor has been with your mother and is still not quite finished. It won't be long. Would you like a cup of tea while you wait?"

Harriet sipped it as she leafed through the Tatler – her mother's favourite since she liked to read all the high society gossip because that's where her daughter's clients came from, only to come across a picture of James Alexander, Rina Cunningham on his arm; she glorious in black, superb against the white skin, the flaming hair. The caption read: *"Mr James Alexander and Miss Rina Cunningham enjoying a joke at the recent Docklands Restoration Ball. Friends say they expect an announcement any day now. Miss Cunningham was formerly married to Mark Terson the racing driver".*

Harriet gazed at the feline face with its great cat's eyes, tip-tilted and glowing, the full sensual mouth, the lush body, and thought: I should imagine she can take her pick from a hundred contenders. Which brings us to the nub of your particular question: What about the one who wants to marry you?

Laying down the magazine she stared into the distance, but there was no way out that she could see. The bottom line was that James Alexander had sussed –

61

how? she thought again, radar? – that she did not want to marry Piers; that she did not want to marry, period, but she had made a promise, and in Harriet's book, a promise was something you kept, no matter what the cost.

And this will cost me all I have, she thought bleakly. I will also be doing what my mother raged against and warned me about all my life: entering into the state of what she termed Unholy Matrimony.

The nurse came back, "Your mother is ready now," and led the way to Mrs Hilliard's door, opening it with a bright: "Look who's here to see you, all the way from London."

Her mother was sitting in a deep armchair by the window, and as she listlessly turned her head Harriet flinched. "Is that you, Harriet?" Mrs Hilliard asked vaguely. "What are you doing home at this hour. You should be at school."

The nurse shook her head before murmuring: "Like I said . . . she had an episode not long after you rang. I'm afraid she is still rather out of it."

You mean drunk, Harriet thought stoically, producing a cheerful voice as she leaned over her mother to say: "How are you, mother?" She smelled soap and talc, both overlying the smell of alcohol.

"I need a drink," Mrs Hilliard whined. "You can get me a bottle of whisky, can't you? I have money . . . my daughter sends it to me, you know. She is very kind is my Harriet." Her face crumpled and her eyes filled. "She would get me a drink . . ."

Harriet looked towards the nurse. "You know you are not supposed to drink, Mrs Hilliard. It is not good for you."

"How do you know what is good for me?" Mrs Hilliard assumed her Queen Dowager mode.

"Look, I've brought you a box of your favourite chocolate Turkish Delight," Harriet said quickly.

Instantly the arrogance turned to greed as Mrs Hilliard accepted the box, tearing at the cellophane wrapping to cram a chocolate into her mouth. "Mmmmm . . . delicious . . ." She smiled up at her daughter. "How kind of you. Did my daughter tell you about me and Turkish Delight? She buys it for me too, you know—"

Harriet looked at the nurse again who said in an undertone: "She comes and goes, bear with her." With an encouraging nod she left the room.

"My daughter is a very successful career girl, you know." Mrs Hilliard went on, fingers questing again even as she talked with her mouth full. "She is an interior decorator – or designer as she says they call them nowadays. She owns her own business and makes a great deal of money. I brought her up to be independent. Never rely on anyone, I told her. They will only let you down. And never, *ever* marry or you will find yourself trapped, as I did." She crammed another chocolate into her mouth. "All the rich and famous ask her to design their houses, you know. She is very successful. And all by her own efforts. Nobody helped her, nobody at all, because I kept telling her nobody ever helps you except with the intention of helping themselves. I wasn't able to do as much as I would have liked because I had no skills, no training, no money, no way out. I married at nineteen and by the time I was twenty I had Harriet and was a prisoner in *his* cage and could do no more than stay and suffer.

My Harriet is a clever girl. Always top of her class at school. She'll go far, her headmistress said to me. I was glad she had ambitions and grateful she had the talent to back them up." Self-pitying tears welled. "All I ever had were the hopes . . ."

"Would you like to go for a walk?" Harriet asked desperately, her own misery not helped by her mother's repeating things Harriet had heard a thousand times before. "It is a lovely day. We can feed the ducks if you like."

Her mother perked. "That would be nice. But I'm not giving them any of my chocolates. They'll have to make do with bread."

Mrs Hilliard allowed herself to be put into the new tweed coat Harriet had bought her, insisting on putting on the hat that went with it before sweeping from the room, still very much the Queen Dowager. The day was a true product of the season; already the bluebells were beginning to flower, making bright splodges against the green of the grass, and the sun was pleasantly warm. After collecting a bag of crusts from the kitchen they made their way down the paths towards the lake, Mrs Hilliard's arm through that of her daughter's for support, for she was unsteady on her feet. Whenever they passed anyone – fellow inmates, visitors, staff, Mrs Hilliard nodded grandly, occasionally announcing – for she had come to recognise her: "This is my daughter Harriet, from London. She is Harriet Hilliard the interior designer, you know."

She fed the swans in the same lordly manner, admonishing them to go on about their business when the supply of bread they had obtained from the kitchen was exhausted. "Just like some people," she observed darkly to Harriet. "Hangers-on for what they can get. I hope you deal sternly with the likes of them. They always hang around successful people. Where are my chocolates?"

"Here."

"I think I will sit down on this bench for a while. Is it clean enough?"

Mrs Hilliard had always been obsessive about cleanliness; it had been one of the bones of contention in the head-tall pile about which she and Harriet's father had argued. In his opinion his wife's relentless cleaning and washing had been over-zealous. Harriet brushed the seat with a tissue but even so, her mother inspected it closely before she sat down. After which, popping another chocolate in her mouth she fell into a light doze.

Seeing the box of Turkish Delight slipping from her lap Harriet reached for it and her mother came to with a start. "No you don't!" she said sharply then: "Why, Harriet . . . they didn't tell me you had come to see me. How nice." Conspiratorially: "Did you bring me something to drink?"

"They won't allow me to."

A sniff. "They won't allow anything in this place." Her smile was sly. "But I have my own little ways . . ." A wink. "Oh, yes . . . I learned how to get round things when *he* was alive. He would never allow me my little drink either. But I knew how to hide it. He would never allow me anything." Vindictively. "He had a heart attack, you know."

"Yes, I know."

"How? Were you at the funeral?"

Her mother was gone again, in and out of reality like a yo-yo. "Yes, I was there."

65

"I enjoyed his funeral. Much better than my wedding. I didn't know what I was in for then, you see." She pursed her lips at Harriet. "I trust you are not married," she said disapprpovingly.

"No."

Mrs Hilliard nodded with satisfaction. "Good. Sensible girl. My Harriet is not married either. I warned her all about that trap. Once a man has you he never lets you go, you know. Life imprisonment is what marriage is and love is what puts you there because emotions enslave. And no bribing the jailer when he is like the one I had. Not that I ever had any money because *he* never gave me any. Such a *mean* man and I never had anything but my looks. That was why he married me. I was very good-looking." Opening the crocodile handbag that had been Harriet's Christmas present a year or so before, Mrs Hilliard took out the pocket mirror. "Now look at me. That's prison pallor, that is." She replaced the mirror, snapped the bag shut. "But he's dead now and I'm free." She helped herself to another chocolate. "I think I'll stay in this place for a while longer. The food's good and anywhere is better than that house because it still reeks of *him* and if I am careful I can have my little drink."

"How do you manage?" Harriet asked casually.

Her mother's look was sly. "Well—" she began, then stopped abruptly as a patient and attendant went slowly by. "Spies," she muttered. "Can't trust anyone, but I'm good at keeping secrets. Kept one from *him* for years. Made myself manage on less than the little he gave me and saved it so as to help my Harriet go to college to learn the skills I could never manage to acquire. That way she could be independent, never have to become any man's slave. And now she is rich and famous and beholden to no one, what I always wanted for her, what I told her time and time and time again to bear in mind. Don't be like me, Harriet. Stay free. Live your life as *you* chose. Marriage is a trap designed by men for men. Love!" Mrs Hilliard's scorn was vitriolic. "It is all a cheat, a lie, a monstrous con. Before I had time to discover what love was I was tied to him and he knew nothing about love, nothing at all. By the time I was twenty I had Harriet so I made her the centre of my life. You must have heard of my Harriet. Harriet Hilliard, the interior designer?"

"Yes. I have heard of her."

"She is very good to me. Bought me this coat, and the hat and the handbag, and she took me away from that horrible house to this lovely place, where there are no reminders of *him*." Turning to the chocolates again: "She brought me these. She knows how I love Turkish Delight."

"Is there anything else you would like her to bring?"

"Yes. A bottle of whisky."

"I am sorry but that is not allowed."

What was left of Mrs Hilliard's once-ravishingly pretty face crumpled. "But I need my little drink . . . it was all I had to keep me going when *he* was alive. It was the only way I could bear him touching me until thank God, he ceased to bother."

Harriet recognised the familiar signs and steered her mother in another direction. "Shall we walk back to the house? I think there are chocolate biscuits for tea."

With alacrity Mrs Hilliard was on her feet. "We had

better get back, then, else there will be none left. There are some greedy people in this place . . ."

Harriet drank a cup of tea while her mother ate her way through several chocolate biscuits and half a chocolate Swiss roll, all the time chanting her own particular mantra: how she had struggled to bring her daughter up 'the right way'.

When Harriet embraced her mother to kiss her goodbye she felt how thin she was, not that she had ever been fat. Harriet had inherited her bone structure: fine-boned and slender. And now it was those bones you felt, while her face, once as lovely as Harriet's, was thin and drawn, her blonde hair grey rather than silver, but styled and set in the way the Queen wore hers. Harriet had never known her mother wear it in any other way. Recognising her daughter once more Mrs Hilliard said briskly: "Now you get back to London and on with your career. Don't worry about me. I am quite happy here. Anywhere is better than *that* house. Make yourself even more successful and me proud by continuing to go it alone. Don't sacrifice what you have achieved on the altar of any man's so-called love. They are all liars. Tell you anything to get what they want. Trust no one and rely on nobody but yourself. That way they can't trap you." Nodding like a Chinese mandarin she returned to her box of chocolates.

As Harriet was leaving the nurse was waiting to tell her that Dr Wilson, the physician in charge of her mother, would like a word with her. When she was sitting opposite his desk he asked: "Which shall it be, good or bad first?"

"I always keep best till last."

"Very well. The bad is that we are having to raise

68

our fees as of next quarter." He told her by how much and Harriet calculated it would cost her another thousand pounds a year to keep mother here. Which I can well afford, she reflected ironically.

"And the good?" she asked.

"Your mother is doing nicely, considering how bad she was when she first came here. Her periods of lucidity are still unpredictable, mostly due to the fact that she is well-advanced in the early stages of arteriosclerosis; that is why her memory comes and goes, as much as the years of drinking. Her brain is not getting its proper blood supply, thus the parts that are deprived are ceasing to function. Which is why it is so vital we keep her alcohol free. Unfortunately, she has been bribing someone to bring her supplies, perhaps one of the delivery men. That is why we would prefer you not to give her money."

"I haven't left her any."

"Good."

"Considering the amount of chocolate she eats she is awfully thin," Harriet observed next.

"That is because she will not eat anything else. And you have to remember she was suffering from severe malnutrition when we accepted her as a patient, not to mention her alcoholic poisoning. We give her vitamin supplements and coax her to eat the things she should, but she would live on nothing but chocolate if she had her way. Whatever she eats, however, she will never be able to live on her own again. She would drink herself to death in a very short time. The one constant in her life is you and her pride in you. That pride is what sustains her, while the whisky helps her escape from memories she hates. But you know already that all alcoholics drink to escape from something or other."

"In my mother's case a disastrously unhappy marriage."

"All your father's fault, according to her."

"Which is not true. They were just – totally unsuited; temperamentally, emotionally, character-wise – every which way. Their constant war of attrition is what killed my father. It just wore him out."

"Yes. It was your mother, in spite of what she says, who was the strong one, in spite of being, as she accuses, trapped, used and manipulated. She was the stronger because she was reinforced by her hatred. She sees herself as the victim but the truth is they were each other's victim."

"I know. I grew up with it."

"You seem to have survived remarkably well."

"I left home when I was eighteen," Harriet told him obliquely.

"Your mother sees your success as her vindication."

Oh, yes. I am good at what I do, Harriet agreed inwardly. In that respect, I have been very successful.

But at nothing else, she thought, as she was driving back to Edgbaston, because I have never known anything else. You can be proud of me as a business-woman, Mother. An independent, beholden to no one career woman with money in the bank and a man who makes no emotional demands as well as few physical ones. Onward and upward, just as you taught me. Self-reliance, Harriet. Self-sufficiency, Harriet. Unto self-obsession? she wondered uneasily. Is that why the thought of sharing my life with Piers does not appeal?

Because to be willing to share your life you first have to love the sharer and love, you warned me, is emotional enslavement. But I do not love Piers, nor do I wish to share my life with him. I have never loved anyone. I don't know how. Did you once love Father? Did you love him so much that when he – as you believed – failed you, that love turned to an equally passionate hate? I don't want that to happen to me. You put the frighteners on me good and proper, Mother. Is it any wonder I took up with a man who posed no threat?

It is not songs my mother taught me, she thought moodily, as she turned into the drive. It is lessons. But God forbid I should end up like you. She thought back to that weekend when she had come home for the first time in what had been a long time to find the usually spotless house filthy and stinking, the food in the cupboards mouldy, the bed fouled and stained and her mother insensibly drunk, the kitchen ankle-deep in empty bottles, most of the cheques Harriet had sent stuffed into a sideboard drawer.

I tried to buy my freedom from you. I left you alone to brood and fester, nursing your hatred because it was all you had. I even lied to Piers and told him you were dead because I wanted that whole part of my life buried along with you. She cut the engine and sat, staring at the now open grave, before being brought back by a rich Edinburgh accent enquiring archly: "I thought it was you, Miss Hilliard, when I saw the car earlier. An expensive new one, isn't it? Been to see your mother, have you? And how is the poor lady? It's a wee while since you were here, isn't it?"

"Mother is fine, thank you."

Mrs McBride clicked her tongue. "Ach, the drink

71

... a terrible thing. Did she know who you were? When I went a while back she didn't know me at all—"

"Yes, she knew me."

"Oh, that's nice, now. I've kept an eye on things for you. Is there anything you are wanting? Will you be staying a few days?"

"No. I have to get back."

"Of course, you have your business to run . . . so proud of you, your mother. Always talking about how successful you are. I had the garden seen to. Nothing gives away an empty house like an untended garden."

"Yes, I noticed," lied Harriet, who had not. "You must let me pay you for that and the next quarter."

She gave Mrs McBride a small cheque every quarter to keep the house up to scratch by cleaning it once a week: just in case her mother ever came back, she had told herself, but really, she understood now, as a bolt-hole for her own needs.

Mrs McBride took the cheque with a satisfied smirk. "I like to think I am being helpful," she conceded self-righteously.

Harriet did not return to London that night. She stopped off at a hotel in Birmingham. The visit to her mother had made her realise she did not want to stay in that whited sepulchre of a house, which had too many reminders she could not cope with right now; like her mother's endless brainwashing and her father's remote silences. He would sit alone cataloguing and re-cataloguing his cases of butterflies – dust collectors, her mother called them, constantly threatening to dispose of them until her quiet, withdrawn husband had said calmly: "The day you dispose of my butterflies, I will dispose of you," and they were never mentioned again.

He had been sitting over them under the green shaded lamp in what was his corner of the living room when he had his coronary, and even then he made no sound so they had not noticed, so used were they to his silence.

Harriet found herself weeping bitterly in bed that night, awash in desolation and despair. Her mother had said, 'You are free, and that was all I ever wanted for you'. Why then, did she she feel she was in solitary confinement?

Five

She was in the shop on the Tuesday morning, talking to a long-standing client, when through the shop window she saw a bright yellow Porsche draw up outside and James Alexander unfold his long length from its interior, bending down to say something to the driver. Harriet saw a white hand come through the open window to rest on the one he had placed on its rim, caught a flash of upturned face, a blaze of hair, then the car shot away down Brook Street. She at once drew the client deeper into the shop; the last thing thing she wanted was to be labelled a Peeping Thomasina, especially since she had decided that her future attitude to James Alexander, whenever she could not avoid him, would be remotely polite, but no more than that.

"Hello, Bert!" James' deep voice expressed surprise as he saw the man Harriet was talking to. "Still playing the Delilah?"

Harriet's lip quivered so she bit it. Bert Kaye – Bertram to his devoted clientele – played the role both ways.

"Watch'er, Jamie-boy! Still pulling the birds?"

"My elastic shows no sign of losing its strength."

Bert giggled. "So I saw . . . Rina back from Paris, then?"

"And hot foot to your clever little hands."

"Then I'd better be off. Wouldn't want to lose a good customer." He turned to Harriet. "Right then, love. You know what I want?"

"And you shall have it."

"I'll leave it all in your own more than capable 'ands. Just send me the bill." He winked at James. "Never puts a foot wrong. I've never 'ad a salon she designed for me fail yet. She's my good-luck piece." He bussed Harriet affectionately on both cheeks, waved a hand at James and was gone.

"From Muswell Hill to Mayfair in sex easy salons," James observed after him.

Harriet almost bit her lip in two.

"I didn't know you knew him," James went on, sounding surprised.

"He was one of my very first clients. What is your excuse?"

"Oh, Bert and I go back a long way . . . only don't ask me where. Now then, I have come to tell you that I have been beavering away on your behalf this weekend. It has to do with a commission."

She eyed him narrowly. Never in a million years would she understand this man. One thing one day, another the next. He raised his eyebrows at her hesitation which had her saying: "Come into the office."

Evelyn was just bringing in coffee. "Light of my life!" exclaimed James. "Just what I need. I have had an exhausting weekend."

Yes, I've just seen her, thought Harriet, but she sat down behind her desk before prompting: "What kind of a commission?"

"A design job in Gloucestershire. Some friends of

mine have just bought themselves a new house. The builders have been in doing some much needed repair and restoration work, but they expect to be finished in a week to ten days, then it is a job from the bare walls up. Corinne – alias Mrs Charles Hervey – saw the house you did for Shuna Meredith and was most impressed. When she mentioned your name I told her I knew you and we went on from there. I sang your praises to such a pretty tune that I am commanded to transport you to Gloucestershire, where the Herveys currently live, for the first available weekend; object, the interior design of Sheringham Court – that's the name of their new house."

Harriet was surprised but not enough to forget her manners. "I am grateful to you for the recommendation."

"Oh, your work was recommendation enough. Corinne buys her dresses from Shuna Meredith, as does another friend of mine."

And no prizes for guessing who that is, Harriet thought, as she leafed through her appointments diary. She and Piers had a theatre and supper engagement on the coming Saturday night but that was easily rearranged; she was otherwise free, and she had always believed in clinching deals as quickly as possible. Any suspicions she had as to James Alexander's reasons in brokering it she would keep to herself for the time being, even if she did watch her back. A commission was a commission was a commission. "I could be free this weekend," she said.

"Ah . . . but I could not. Shall we say the weekend after?"

If you must, Harriet thought, feeling her adrenalin

subside reluctantly. "All right," she agreed, making the necessary entry.

"Good. I'll pick you up on the Friday afternoon – say around three?" Innocently: "It will be all right with Piers, I trust?"

Harriet just looked at him.

He held out his cup. "Could I have a refill?"

As she was pouring her phone rang. "It's Lady Anstey," Evelyn said in warning tones. "Abut that Tiffany lamp . . ."

Harriet groaned inwardly. Lady Anstey was a lucrative client but a difficult one. "Put her on," she said, then, to James: "Do you mind?"

"Yes, but would it make any difference?" He took himself off.

Harriet spent a good fifteen minutes soothing Lady Anstey, promising to change the lamp, knowing full well it would eventually be changed back again. All the client wanted to do was make her presence felt.

No sooner had she put the phone down than it rang again, and this time it was an irate painter-decorator who was being held up for lack of the special, hand-blocked paper he was to hang. Harriet calmed him down then made mincemeat of the supplier, after which, feeling in the mood, she gave short shrift to an upholsterer who had covered a set of six Victorian chairs in the wrong shade of velvet. While she was about it she next laid into the man who handmade her lampshades because he had supplied her with two shoddy examples of his work.

Feeling, for some reason she could not specify, in the mood for battle, she sailed into the shop ready to deal with James Alexander only to find he had gone. "A luncheon appointment," Evelyn sighed enviously. "A Miss Cunningham."

Which left Harriet with a full head of steam and no one to vent it on until a client – for whom she had already resolved never to work again – came in to complain about being supplied a K'ang horse lamp-base he said was cracked, demanding Harriet replace it. Demanding recompense, he found Harriet so icily polite, so skin-strippingly disbelieving that he retreated in considerable disorder, resolving to tell his wife – who had herself cracked the damn thing – to do her own dirty work in future.

Harriet went to her own luncheon appointment high on adrenalin, and coming back down Bond Street was stopped dead in her tracks by a dress in the window of Rive Gauche.

Adrift in a cloud of ruffles, it foamed delicately: a froth of sea-green organza. Buy me! it commanded. So she did. But during a flat, dull afternoon, going over accounts with Miss Judd, in spite of their highly satisfactory state Harriet found her own spiritual soufflé sinking, and when she got home that night looked at the dress and thought: I must have been mad. What on earth possessed me? Ruffles! Organza! Not me at all. Her taste ran to line and cut rather than indeterminate drifts of masculine-oriented femininity. She hung it right at the back of her wardobe. That will teach you to give way to impulse, she told herself grimly.

On the Friday of the weekend she was due to go into Gloucestershire, she went to Bert's Knightsbridge salon to have her hair done. Bert always attended to her himself, and sitting under his expert scissors she could not help but remember what James had said about him.

"Now that's a cat's got-the-cream smile," Bert observed cheekily. "Goin' somewhere nice, are we?"

"Shan't know until I get there."

"Business or pleasure?"

"Business I hope will turn out to be a pleasure."

"Don't we all?" he enquired archly before going back to his cutting. After a while: "I didn't know you knew Jamie-boy."

"Not as well as you do, obviously. I've never heard anyone else call him Jamie, but I know him because he helped me out at the shop."

Clicking his tongue: "I'eard you was under the weather. 'Ad a nice rest, did yer? In the sun by the looks of that tan. I'm a sun worshipper meself; brings out the beast in me – and on the beaches, come to that . . ."

Harriet laughed at his saucy grin.

"So Jamie-boy helped you out, did he? Not surprising. He has a nifty pair of hands when it comes to helping women. Watch yourself, ducks. He's fly as any mosquito. I could tell you the names of some as has come down with malaria that'd surprise you."

"I doubt it."

"Got 'is number, 'ave yer? That makes a change. 'E usually 'as yours. Mind you, with the bird as is in 'is cage at the moment 'e does have both 'ands full, so to speak. Hoity-toity madam she is and no mistake. Comes in here like she's Gods gift to the male libido!" Bert gave one of his sniffs; it spoke volumes. "I

80

wouldn't 'ave 'er if she was gift-wrapped. Nasty bit of work when she's crossed – like 'er eyes."

Harriet giggled.

"Straight up! Blind as a bat without 'er contacts. Lost one of them in 'ere one day and acted like we'd done it deliberate. 'Ad to take the other one out and be led away. Laugh! I couldn't cut straight. Swore us all to secrecy, she did, which I did with everythin' crossed but me own eyes. Snooty bitch, but a rare looker, I'll grant you that. Jamie-boy's birds is always top-cream." He shook his head in admiration. "That one could topple a vestal virgin. The things I could tell you! Don't give a tinker's damn, but a rare friend. Been a good one to me and no mistake. Got me out of a spot of bother once (which I won't go into seein' as you are a lady as was gently reared) but 'e went out on a limb for me and I set great store by that. You could bet your life on Jamie Alexander and still get best odds."

"As a matter of fact," Harriet found herself saying, "I am going, off for the weekend with him this very afternoon – strictly business", she added quickly in the face of Bert's dropped jaw.

"Just so long as you watch 'e don't give it to you. 'E's got more mileage than a vintage Rolls and you're not – if you'll pardon the expression – 'is type of bird. Not that 'e 'asn't 'ad just about every species in the book – and I don't mean the Guinness Book of Records, neither."

"I will keep both eyes open at all times."

"And your door locked – not that 'e wouldn't come through the window. 'E's done that before 'an all . . ."

Harriet mopped her streaming eyes. "What hasn't he done?" she managed.

81

"Nothin' – and nobody. The things I could tell you; things 'as was told to me by women in this very chair. They don't need no curlers when e's around, believe me."

He stood back before saying: "There now, 'ow's that?"

"Perfect," Harriet said truthfully. Her hair gleamed, short and thick and bouncy, framing her oval face.

"Still usin' my shampoo and conditioner?"

"Faithfully. I'll have a further supply while I'm here."

"My pleasure."

"Oh, no," Harriet said feelingly, "it's been mine."

James picked her up promptly at three o'clock. He was dressed for the country: beautifully cut cavalry twill trousers and a shirt checked in green, yellow and brown under a soft cashmere sweater the colour of pistachio nuts. As it was a mild, early May day his jacket lay on the back seat.

Settling herself in the front seat Harriet could smell perfume . . . sultry and sexy. Not one she could identify nor one she would wear. Too heavy. She wound the window down.

"Sure it won't be too breezy for you?" James asked, and as she met his eyes she knew that he knew why.

"I like fresh air," she told him.

"I would hate that brand new hairdo to be blown to blazes. Bert Kaye? His scissors are unmistakable."

"Yes."

James smiled. "He's a character. Sterling, in spite of the baroque finish. Does he give you a run down on the latest unprintables as he cuts?"

"Today was not unprintable. Just – highly informa-
tive."

She felt his sharp glance. 'I can imagine. He must
keep more secrets than the KGB. Do you tell him
yours?"

"None to tell."

"Not that you would, anyway. What do you do,
confide them to your diary?"

"Don't keep one – except for business appointments."

"Of course. Everything locked away in that head of
yours, like Fort Knox. What do you call that colour
anyway? Guinea-gold? And on the subject of colour,
contrary to popular opinion, I am not as black as I am
painted. Did Bert do a Dorian Gray?"

"You flatter yourself."

"I'd much rather flatter you."

He drove for a while in silence, hands negligently on
the wheel, one elbow resting on the open window. He
wore no rings; only a wafer-thin gold watch on a plain
leather strap. "You don't like me, do you," he said,
making a statement rather than asking a question.

"I don't see what that has to do with anything,"
Harriet answered obliquely.

"Of course it does. I believe in making friends and
influencing people."

"Really! And there was me thinking it was the other
way round."

"Watch it," he said cheerfully, "your straight laces
are showing."

"So I am old-fashioned. I am not ashamed to wear
them."

"But not as a flag of convenience."

Something in his tone had her wariness sighting along its barrel. "Never. And only in my own colours."

"Which suit you no end. You once told me I must make allowances. Don't you think it is time you ran up a few of your own?"

"I am not much of a hand with a needle," Harriet lied, only to be floored when he countered:

"That's no feather you have been stitching me up with."

She had believed him too heavily armoured in self-esteem to feel her small pin-pricks. It made her say, with mock hunility: "Oh, I am sorry. It was not intentional."

"Of course it was. You have been busy with your needle from the moment we met. Why? What have I ever done to you?"

"How about interfered in my private life?" It was out before she could stop it.

"Ah . . . Paula and her American Croesus. What did I do? Wake the dead?"

"If you will blow your own trumpet—"

"But not in your orchestra, is that it? And you a one-woman band. Listen to yourself a moment, Harrict. It is time you changed your tune."

"Piers likes it."

"Piers wouldn't know the difference between Strauss and Sondheim. He's tone-deaf. Fancy you not knowing that." His 'tut-tut' had Harriet grinding her teeth. It was something she had indeed not known. She had never discussed music with Piers.

"Still, as long as he continues to dance to your tune it makes no mind."

"With all the strings you have to your bow I am sure

you are able to make any tune you play sound like the sirens' song," Harriet shot back nastily.

He threw back his head and laughed with unaffected enjoyment. "No wonder Piers is punch-drunk. You pack a hefty wallop for a small bundle."

"Never laid a finger on him!"

"Just as well. He would be out of his class."

Her tones as chill as a well-frosted Margarita: "Contrary to popular opinion, my relationship with Piers is in no way a fifteen round contest for the Championship of the World."

"But I thought you had already won that? Taken it by the horns, thrown and hog-tied it." Then so swiftly that she did not feel the knife: "Which makes me wonder why on earth you did not do the same thing to Paula years ago . . . If you had, there would have been absolutely no need for me to 'interfere' as you told me in no uncertain terms."

"I can still manage without your contribution, thank you."

"Surely that depends on the value you put on Piers."

"I am very well aware of *his* worth, thank you."

"Such a contumacious female."

"Better that than an inconsistent one."

"Oh, I do not doubt for a moment that you have been entirely faithful to Piers – in your fashion."

"I know what suits me."

"And if it does not suit Piers?"

"If it did not he would have taken himself off long ago."

"But where has he got to go?"

Harriet drew in a sharp breath. "If this is how you make friends then you don't need any enemies!"

85

"I make a very bad enemy."

Something in his voice had her asking: "Is that a warning?"

"Take it any way you like."

"There is only one thing I am prepared to take as far as you are concerned."

"And what might that be?" He sounded interested.

"Umbrage!"

His grin was huge. "Oh, Harriet, you are something else. No wonder you've got Piers wandering around in a daze."

"Just so long as you remember at all times that I am not!"

For some reason the argument was a hypo of pure adrenalin, resulting in her feeling almost intoxicatingly exhilarated. She had not enjoyed such a verbal battle in an age. Piers was no gladiator. Always gave in without a fight. This man was a championship opponent. She waited with gleeful anticipation for his next move, but when it came it floored her.

"It is what you are not which interests me," he said.

Harriet moved speedily to block that dangerous turn-off. "I assure you, Mr Alexander, there is no need for you to interest yourself in me in the first place." Pause, then with emphatic deliberation: "It is not as though I have any interest in you. We no longer need to work together so we can both go our separate ways."

"And you can have *Harriet Designs* all to yourself. I hope you will be very happy together. Just so long as you remember that bigamy is a punishable offence. But that is why you are in no hurry to marry Piers, isn't it? It is not his divorce which is holding things up. It is your own, indissoluble union with your alter ego."

Harriet had to struggle to find the breath to say when she could: "Leave my motives out of this, if you please. Yours are the ones I suspect. Like just why you have got your hands placed firmly in the small of Piers' back!"

"Because he is one of my oldest friends to whom I once inadvertently did a wrong turn. And because he is so obviously fed-up with hanging around. You have had him in cold-storage so long he is all but petrified –" he moved in to administer the *coup de grâce* "– of you as well as by you."

"That's a lie!" It was automatic because Harriet was gazing in horror at what had crawled out from under the stone he had just turned over.

"Think about it." He was unyielding. "If you really wanted Piers (and that is something else you know nothing about, by the way) the fires of hell would be as a damp squib to a woman of your drive and capabilities. Piers is a front: one you hide behind while you get on with what really matters to you – *Harriet Designs*."

Harriet's face had leached, and she felt she was leaking blood all over his expensive leather upholstery but in a voice stripped to the bone she said: "That is it! The absolute end! If it was not that it would be very bad manners I would make you stop this car, turn it around and drive me back to town. I'd as soon as go to hell rather than into Gloucestershire with you. No, I do not like you! I never will like you! You are an arrogant, interfering know-it-all who thinks he is God's gift to the female sex and thus has *carte blanche* to rearrange their private lives. I don't care how old a friend you are to Piers, you are no friend of mine! Get off my back, Mr Alexander. I have no intention of allowing you to be my Old Man of the Sea!"

"Bravo!" He was not in the least put out. "You have just confirmed my every opinion of you, Harriet. And for the rest of the way you can sit and think about whatever they might be." He must have put his foot down, because the car surged forward, the countryside rushing past in a blur.

The hell I will! was Harriet's incandescent reaction. Your opinions are of no interest to me, Mr Alexander. What you think and what I believe haven't been so much as introduced!

"Except", her sly demon insinuated, 'where this particular commission is concerned. It is on his re-commendation you are in line for it in the first place. He carries a lot of clout, and we want him to use it on your behalf rather than clobber you with it. If you know what is good for *Harriet Designs* you will mend those trampled fences. Right now you need this man, loathe him though you might, so belay the belligerence and mind your manners.'

Biting her lip: "I'm sorry," she apologised, stiff as a corpse. "I lost my temper."

"You do seem to have a hard time reining it in around me. I wonder why—"

"Please . . ." Harriet had acknowledged her need, she was damned if she was going to let him needle her into another outburst. "Let's change the subject, shall we? Tell me about your friends the Herveys . . ."

Six

The Herveys' house, Fairlawns, lay at the bottom of the hill that formed the main street of a lovely old Cotswold village. After navigating the massive chestnut tree that formed a natural roundabout, they drove through a wide-open five-barred gate onto a gravelled drive, tyres crunching. Through overhanging trees Harriet caught glimpses of a square, sturdy house built of Cotswold stone, with mullioned windows and a wide expanse of lawns beneath shallow terraces. She could hear children, and as the house came into full view she saw two small boys playing on a swing placed on the flagged terrace.

James stopped the car in front of it and the boys likewise stopped what they were doing to see who had arrived. When they did they uttered whoops of joy and flung themselves in his direction.

"Uncle James!" They exhibited the kind of uninhibited delight which indicated a very welcome visitor. As he got out of the car they hurled themselves at him, he protesting laughingly but accepting their hugs, returning them in good measure. Just then, a woman's voice called:

"James? Is that you? Shan't be a minute."

Shading her eyes against the afternoon sun, Harriet saw that a stable yard lay facing the house, and it was from there that the voice had come. As she gazed, she saw a stable door open and a Junoesque blonde in jodphurs and a well-filled canary yellow sweater, a match to her hair, come out of it. Shutting it carefully behind her she reached up to pat the muzzle of the big black horse which nudged her neck as she did so.

"All right, all right . . . you shall have your apple," Harriet heard her say in a besotted voice, and watched as she reached down to the basket by the door to take out an apple which she proffered on the flat of her palm. The horse delicately covered it for a moment before lifting his head, leaving the palm bare as he crunched contentedly. "Greedy . . ." the blonde said, in a voice that belied the scold. With a last pat she came across to where the boys were fighting for first place with James, while Harriet stood by.

"Boys, please! Do leave James in one piece!" she ordered, before embracing him herself. "Lovely to see you," she said, "and this must be Miss Hilliard." Smilingly she thrust out a hand. "Welcome to Fairlawns. I'm Corrine Hervey. I'm so glad you could come."

Harriet shook her hostess's hand. "Thank you. I am happy to be here."

"Have a good journey down?" Corinne asked James.

"Somewhat bumpy," James admitted, in a way that had her eyeing him in surprise.

"But there aren't any road works . . . Oh!" Her eyes sparkled. "I see – you struck out!" Turning to Harriet. "I can see you and I are going to get along splendidly. It is not often I get to meet one of the vanquishers rather than the vanquished. Take in the bags will you,

James? You are in your usual room; I've put Miss Hilliard in the gold room. Goes with your colouring," she told Harriet admiringly. "Now, come along and have some tea and tell me how you came to give James, of all people, a bumpy ride."

Corinne led Harriet into the house, through a wide square hall lit by a large mullioned window on the first landing which, being of stained glass, shed pools of multi-coloured light on a highly polished parquet floor, and down a short corridor into a small sitting room filled with afternoon sunshine and overlooking the terrace where the boys had gone back to their playing. Drawn up in front of the carved stone firelace was a butler's tray laid with silver teapot and spirit kettle, Wedgewood china, a plate of freshly made sandwiches, another of oven-warm scones, with accompanying jam and cream, and a third of chocolate cake.

The furniture was comfortable: a vast leather Chesterfield with matching armchairs, a beautiful Regency bookcase overflowing with a motley collection, a small but exquisite secretaire littered with papers, an old but beautifully polished Georgian sofa table piled with magazines, several Sheraton chairs which Harriet noted as badly in need of re-upholstering, and a triangular Chinese cabinet filled with matching porcelain. On the grey stone of the mantelpiece, almost hidden by a thicket of invitations, was a series of small Victorian fairings in black and white glazed ware.

"Do sit down," Corinne invited, going to what was her accustomed place behind the spirit kettle. "I expect you are dying for a cuppa – especially after your bumpy ride." Her eyes, the vivid blue of gentians, were alight with gleeful curiosity.

"You are American, aren't you?" Harriet asked, heading her off at the pass.

"Born and bred in Virginia but married in England to an Englishman."

"How long?"

"Ten years."

"So you are an old friend of Mr Alexander's?"

"Oh, we go all the way back to childhood. His mother and mine are cousins." Her eyes twinkled as she went on: "I must tell you that to them, James is known as The One Who Got Away, but he did me the greatest favour of my life by introducing me to Charles, so I count myself fortunate." Measuring tea from a silver caddy: "Mind you, James is a dab hand at bestowing old flames where they will warm the most."

Harriet thought bitterly of Paula Cayzer just as a deep voice asked: "Well, aren't you the light of my life?" and she turned to see an enormous man stoop to come through the door. He could not have been less than six and a half feet tall (she learned later than it was six feet seven inches) and built on a Herculean scale. Below a thatch of hair as lint-white as that of his two sons outside was a craggy face out of which two ice-blue eyes regarded Harriet with both interest and curiosity. He wore rumpled cord trousers and was rolling down the sleeves of his Tattersall check shirt over arms as thick as her thighs.

"Darling, just in time. Come and meet Miss Hilliard." Corrine's smile was deeply affectionate. "You'll be paying her fee, after all."

He came across to shake hands. "My wife and I saw

92

what you did for Shuna Meredith and were most impressed. Corinne said at once that you were the one to do up our new house."

"Indeed," Corinne agreed. "Shuna's house is a dream, but then, she has some lovely pieces. Still, you gave them the perfect setting. Do you think you can do the same for us?"

"I'm sure I can. I notice you have some lovely pieces of your own."

Corrine's smile was gratified. "I am no expert but I do know something about furniture and porcelain – thanks to James, who knows it all. He has kept me from being taken in by the cleverest of fakes."

Harriet felt that one like a blow.

"I believe he helped you out for a while when you were under the weather?" Charles sympathised, seating himself on the huge Chesterfield, no doubt the reason for its oversize.

"My doctor thought I needed some R&R," Harriet threw away. "Now that I have had it there is no further need for Mr Alexander to concern himself – though I am grateful, of course, for his recommendation to you."

Corinne began to pour the tea, but glanced at Harriet from under her lashes, caught by something in her tone. Just then, the subject of the conversation joined them

It was obvious to Harriet from the start that he occupied a special place in this particular household, and her impression was confirmed when, the adults having finished their tea, the two small boys, newly washed and brushed, were led in by their Nanny.

Both were beautiful children, with their father's hair and their mother's eyes. James, the eldest aged eight, was named for his godfather, while Jeremy was six. He it was, after expertly sizing up the situation, who decided to focus himself on Harriet, turning his gentian eyes on her in such a way as to make her murmur *sotto voce* to his mother: "God help the women in twenty years if he looks at them like that."

"Don't let him get away with anything," warned Corinne, obviously pleased. "He is a shameless opportunist."

"Oh, I know all about them," Harriet said, looking straight into James Alexander's shimmering eyes.

"Would you like to see my pony?" Jeremy asked beguilingly. "His name is Buttons."

"That would be nice."

"Have you got a pony?"

"No. I only once rode a horse – a donkey rather – and that was on the beach at Bognor. I prefer Shank's pony."

"Who is he?"

"Now you've done it," Corinne warned. "He will give you no peace until you explain it all to his satisfaction."

"You can tell me when you come upstairs to say good-night," Jeremy commanded, in absolutely no doubt that Harriet would.

They sat on talking, while the boys were each allowed a scone and a piece of Devil's food cake – "My great-grandmother's recipe," Corinne told Harriet – and to bring in Shep, the big golden Labrador, who was given his own piece of chocolate cake, and William, the white Pekinese, who preferred bread and butter. Shep was affable and proffered Harriet a paw; William came to sniff but did not stay; he was a one-woman dog and that woman was Corinne.

After about forty minutes, Nanny came back again to take the boys upstairs for bath, supper and bed.

Rising to her feet, Corinne said: "I'll take you upstairs Harriet – I may call you Harriet?" Her smile was warm. "We Americans tend to use first names from first introductions – and show you where your room is. This house has been added to periodically over the past two hundred and fifty years with the result that it is a bit of a rabbit warren. It was originally a farmhouse and the one thing that was kept was the kitchen, which is the size of a barn, but at least it meant I could install an American fridge. How you British ever manage with those Lilliputian ice-boxes of yours I will never know . . ."

Harriet's room was delightful; all gold and cream, glazed cotton and diamond-paned windows.

"If you need a guide to bring you down for dinner, James is just across the hall," Corinne told her.

Harriet smiled, resolving to do no such thing. Going to the window she looked out. "Oh, how pretty . . ." The view was of rolling hills sloping to a valley at the bottom where a river meandered, and up the other side to a village with a church steeple. Cows were dotted around the fields like pins in a green baize board, and there were horses grazing everywhere, as well as sheep.

"Yes, isn't it?" Corinne agreed. "Reminds me of home. You ever been to Virginia?"

"I have never even been to America." Piers had always been wary about Harriet accompanying him on his frequent trips there; the very thing to start all the

95

tongues wagging, he had said from pursed lips, so she had never got to go.

"Oh, then you must – you absolutely *must*. If you like this you'd love Tidewater country."

"How can you bear to leave it all?" Harriet gestured to the view.

"Because I need more space for my beauties – my hunters. Like a good Virginian, my passion is horses. Do you hunt?"

"Only for the right bibelots."

"Pity . . . this is Heythrop country. So what is your hobby?"

"My work."

"James told us you have a drive like a camshaft." American-direct in her curiosity: "What happened to make you give him a bumpy ride? Do tell!"

"Merely a difference of opinion." In the face of Corrine's obvious scepticism: "I hardly know him," Harriet felt constrained to add. "He is a friend of my partner, not of mine."

"You mean Piers Cayzer."

"You know Piers?"

"Yes, he was at school with Charles." Interestedly: "Tell me, how did James do as your . . . locum?"

"From a distance you would never know," Harriet replied non-comittally.

Corinne's eyes sparkled. "I knew it! Every other female James has brought down here has been eating out of his hand. Something tells me you bit it. Why?"

"Mr Alexander and I are business acquaintances, no more," Harriet said with crisp and absolute finality. "Do not look for me on the roll of the honoured laid."

Corinne fell back on the bed, whooping with laughter. "Oh, boy! James said you had a tongue like an asp. I've always hoped to see the day when he met his match. I've seen so many go up in flames. Still, he was already pipped at the post by Piers. How is he, these days? We haven't seen him in an age."

"He is fine, thank you."

"You know it was James who introduced him to Paula." Eyeing Harriet's closed face Corrine went on shrewdly: "Is that what you have against him?"

"It was Piers who married her," Harriet pointed out.

"True." Corrine got up from the bed. She knew when it was futile to continue to probe. Ten years in England had taught her that while Americans did not think twice about offering up their life histories on being introduced, expecting the same frankness in return, the English regarded such instant confidences as over-familiarity. "I must go and see to things. If you want the nursery you go up the stairs at the end of this corridor, straight along the passage and through the door at the end. Up the second flight of stairs and you are there."

When she had unpacked and bestowed her various bits and pieces in the very American bathroom, Harriet followed her instructions and found Jeremy already sitting up in bed, an expectant look on his face.

"I knew you would come," he said simply.

"Oh, you are going to cut such a swathe . . ." Harriet sighed, meeting the limpid blue eyes.

"What does that mean?"

"You will have a great time finding out."

Patting his bed as an invitation to Harriet to sit down: "Would you like to read me a story now?"

97

"Do I have a choice?"

"Yes. Any one you like."

Harriet laughed. "Already a slippery customer. All right . . . is this the book you want? *Grimms' Fairy Tales*?" She riffled through the pages only to have Jeremy put a hand on an illustration.

"That one . . . the Queen looks like you."

"The Snow Queen?"

"Yes. She has yellow hair and blue eyes."

And ice for a heart? Harriet thought uncomfortably.

"The resemblance doesn't end there," James Alexander's voice confirmed, and looking round Harriet saw him leaning against the door jamb, his namesake peering from under his arm. "Go on," he urged, "read us all a story. After all, you do believe in fairytales, don't you?"

For a moment their eyes met and held, then Harriet looked back down at the book in her lap, controlling her sudden spurt of rage. What was it with this bloody man? He had accused her of wielding the needle but he would have made a fine surgeon himself.

Sauntering in, both Jameses sat down on the window seat. "All right," the Senior announced. "We are all sitting comfortably. You may begin."

Harriet had no choice but to do so. She had not read aloud for years; not since she used to read long stretches of Trollope and Dickens to her father when his eyes began to go, and at first she was constrained by her prickling awareness of James Alexander's looming presence, but as she warmed to the story of Gerda and Kay she lost herself in it and relaxed, and when Jeremy nestled against her she put an arm around him, feeling the soft child-warmth of him, smelling of bath-

98

time and innocence. She was unaware that her audience was under her spell, their silence so total that Nanny came to investigate – and stayed to listen.

When Harriet finished the story: "I felt sorry for the poor Snow Queen," Jeremy pronounced.

"I liked Kay and Gerda better," his brother differed. "I wouldn't let any old Snow Queen put ice in *my* eyes."

"All the better to freeze you with," his godfather pointed out.

"Now say good-night and thank you to Miss Hilliard," Nanny ordered benignly, stout and placid and thirty years experienced in the ways of children.

"Harriet will tuck me in won't you Harriet?" Jeremy said sweetly.

"Miss Hilliard to you, my lad," James said in the voice of authority, which prompted Harriet to say at once: "You may call me Harriet, Jeremy. All my friends do."

"Uncle James will tuck me in, won't you?" his namesake said as he climbed into the other bed, determined not to be outdone.

When Jeremy was bestowed to his satisfaction, which meant nice and tight, he said: "And a good-night kiss," but when she bent to him he threw his arms around her in a bearhug. "Tomorrow I will take you to see Buttons."

"I look forward to that." She stood smiling down at him until James said:

"If you ever decide to give up being a designing woman you could always make a good living doing *A Book at Bedtime*."

Brushing past him she went back downstairs, he following, but at her own door she turned, wearing a smile that had him raising his eyebrows. "I know the very thing to read to you," she promised, in way that had him asking immediately:

"Oh? What?"

"The Riot Act."

Whisking through her door she shut it in his face.

For some reason Annie had packed the confection of sea-green ruffles as well as the plain black crepe dinner dress Harriet had specified. An old favourite, it was a Jean Muir piece of perfection, starkly plain but of superb cut, with a pleated bodice which hugged her narrow rib-cage and moulded her small but firm high breasts before falling straight and clean to just above her ankles. Its long sleeves were tight to show off her elegant forearms and wrists, while its neckline was a deep V, at the base of which Harriet pinned one, single, creamy camelia, which she took from the vase on her dressing table.

Hanging the dress behind the door to remove any slight creases, she took a long, leisurely bath, feeling a smug sense of satisfaction at having – firmly and decisively – put that infuriating James Alexander in his place. She did her face with care, and brushing her hair noted contentedly that it fell into place just as Bert had said it would. She sprayed *Amarige* liberally before donning her dress, slid her feet into plain black pumps and picked up her envelope-type evening bag, both of the same material as her dress. One last 360-degree turn in front of the mirror told her all was well before she went downstairs.

She had memorised the route by mental markers. Past the magnificent Chinese sandalwood chest, across the landing where the Corot hung, down the staircase to where the Charles II cabinet stood against a plain white wall, down the right-hand corridor past the Jacobean settle and onto the main landing. As she reached the hall she heard music, and following her ear, came to a partly open door through which she could see Charles Hervey taking up most of the room on a Knole sofa uphlolstered in crushed-rose velvet. He rose to his feet as she entered. The room was large, a sea of polished parquet scattered with exquisite rugs and small islands of furniture, all dominated by a superb Bechstein grand on which was scattered a collection of jade animal miniatures. A fine pair of Chippendale sidetables faced each other on opposite walls under matching mirrors fitted with candle sconces, and there was more fine porcelain exhibited in illuminated shell cabinets in each corner. The fireplace was a massive slab of Cotswold stone under a canopy, and it was filled with an arrangement of leaves, ferns and berries. A regimental base drum served as a table and it bore an arrangement of bottles and glasses. The whole was being serenaded by Mozart.

"No need to send out the Saint Bernard, then, or should I say the Saint James."

"I have a very good sense of direction," Harriet returned lightly, refusing to be drawn by the twinkle in his eyes. Obviously Corinne had told him All, and she knew by now that both Herveys were incorrigible teases.

"Come and sit down. What would you like to drink? A gin and tonic? I can make an American martini – my wife showed me how – or I have some excellent dry sherry . . ."

"Sherry, please." Harriet had heard of the American

Dry Martini. According to Piers it was their Most Lethal Weapon, and around James Alexander she needed her wits in full working order. She seated herself on a chair whose seat had been exquisitely embroidered in *gros point* in a flower pattern. "This is lovely," she admired.

"My wife's handiwork."

"I see that Mrs Hervey is a lady of many talents."

Handing her a *copita* of pale sherry: "I trust you find us equable enough to address as Charles and Corinne. I already think of you as Harriet. Such a charming, old-fashioned name. It suits you."

"In that I am charming or old-fashioned?"

"Charming, certainly, old-fashioned – well, not to look upon or talk to, but in no way the state-of-the-art career woman James had led us to expect."

His eyes were twinkling again, in such a way that Harriet could not be sure if he was teasing or not, but she thought it as well to say – and amusedly: "Do not believe all you hear from Mr Alexander."

"Oh, I know him well enough not to, but I do owe him for introducing you to us. I am sure you will do us proud."

"Where is your new house?"

"In a village about three miles from here, as the crow flies; about five by road. We'll take a run over tomorrow morning. Tomorrow afternoon it is our current village May Fayre and I have no doubt Corinne will co-opt you into serving behind her White Elephant stall. She has an eye for spotting what will sell and up until now, every year she has sold out. We have spent ten very happy years in this village, but needs must, and Caroline's need is for bigger stables and more grazing for her horses. If our new village is as friendly as this one has been then we shall indeed be fortunate."

Coming along the passage, Corinne found James at the mirror by the drawing room door, fussing with his black tie. "What's the matter? Having trouble?"

"This is just not my day," he sighed.

"Turn around . . ."

He did so, and it gave him the opportunity to look through the not quite closed door of the drawing room to where Harriet, elbow on knee, chin on hand, was leaning forward, absorbedly listening to Charles expound on the problems that beset the present day farmer. The matt cameo of her profile was etched against the warm rosy glow of the walls, and the folds of her dress fell about her, like the drapery of a statue. Following his eyes as she gave his tie a last pat, Corinne said: "Struck out there, did you, James? She is charming, and very lovely, but a little – too . . . got together, don't you think? Keeps her tongue well honed too. And how clever to wear black."

"Harriet is a very clever girl."

"Who has set her sights elsewhere, and tell me pray, how come such a dull old stick as Piers Cayzer managed to hook such a prize?"

"He didn't. She hooked him."

"Oh? I would have thought she did well enough on her own without having to dig for money."

"It is not his money she is after. Whatever Harriet is – and I am still finding my way through that particular maze – she is no Paula."

Corinne's eyes positively glittered.

"Down, girl," James advised with the familiarity of

103

long friendship. "All will be revealed in due course. Just possess your kindly old soul in patience." Pushing open the drawing room door he said: "Now then you two . . . no starting the party without us . . ."

Seven

O n the Saturday morning, after a leisurely breakfast, they all drove over to the new house. It was
a Queen Anne gem, set four square at the straight edge
of a half-moon drive, terraces falling away at the rear
to a sunken garden, while the stables occupied a
handsome block all to themselves, built around a
magnificent yard, complete with arch and clock.

It was Jeremy who took Harriet by the hand and led
her round, especially to the rooms right at the top of
the house destined to become the nursery. Large enough to take three children, for Corinne had told
Harriet she was expecting her third child in October.

"I only hope it is the girl Charles longs for. I'm
damned if I am giving up hunting another year!"

"You are very lucky," Harriet said sincerely.

"I know." Then in her usual teasing fashion: "Better
get your skates on, Harriet. If you go on waiting for
Piers much longer you will be too old to have your own
children! I would never have the patience. Couldn't
you find yourself a guy with a loose rein? I would have
a thought a girl with your looks would have had them
beating a path to your door."

Which brought to mind what James had said about
being married to her job. Now, with Jeremy's small
hand in hers, she realised that she would like a child of

her own. She liked children; always had. It was just that her ambitions had held pride of place for so long everything else had perforce been put in her 'Pending' folder; part of a 'one day, some day', proposal. But then, as she was belatedly coming to realise, her personal filing cabinet was crammed with far too many of those.

As they went round the house Harriet took measurements and notes, paced out floors, discussed colour schemes and sounded out Corrine's preferences as well as what Charles wanted for his own study. By the end of the morning they were well satisfied with each other. Corinne knew she would get what she wanted, Charles was happy because she was happy, and Harriet satisfied because she would have the free hand she liked.

After lunch, they all walked up to the green at the top of the village, where the May Fayre was to be held. It was opened promptly at three o'clock by the wife of the local Squire, after which Harriet, as Charles had warned, was pressed into service at Corinne's White Elephant stall, which was cleared by half-past four, to the tune of a very satisfying profit which would, along with the rest of the proceeds of the afternoon, go towards the restoration of the organ in the Parish Church. Leaving Corinne to gloat over her success with the rest of her committee, Harriet went to to join Jeremy, who had waited for her patiently, on a tour of the funfair.

She rode with him on the roundabout, swung on the swings, shied balls at coconuts, rolled pennies and fished for goldfish, enjoying every moment of it. She even engaged in a bumper-to-bumper duel on the dodgems with the two Jameses, causing Corinne to observe to her husband as they watched: "Harriet is a different girl when she lets her hair down."

"It's hardly long enough; short and blunt, like her."

"You know what I mean. She is so . . . got together I get the feeling it would take a blowtorch to dismantle her."

"You mean James," her husband said dryly.

"Can you think of anyone better? Except for some reason he has got absolutely nowhere."

"How do you know? What proof have you that he's even tried? Tone down the colour on that imagination of yours and whatever you do don't start matchmaking again. Your name is Corrine Hervey not Emma Woodhouse, the only resemblance being that like her, not a single one of your efforts has succeeded in getting James to the altar. Besides, Harriet is spoken for, as you well know."

"By a dried-up stick like Piers Cayzer! Why, is what I'd like to know. She could make mincemeat of him."

"Perhaps she likes mincemeat."

"No." Corinne shook her head decisively. "There is more here than meets the eye, but I'm damned if I can get James to tell me where to look."

"Good. Leave it alone, Corinne. It is none of our business."

"But Harriet is so right for James, surely you saw it at once? She has spirit and brains and gives as good as she gets. You know he gets bored with sugar-water after a while. Harriet is triple distilled, one hundred per cent pure alcohol."

"Are you sure you are not just after revenge?" teased

her husband. "Just because he once had his ring through your nose . . ."

"And who has it tight in his hand right now? I'm only trying to repay the favour he did when he introduced me to you."

"Then repay it by not meddling. It only leads to trouble."

But Corinne was gazing at Harriet with a pensive glint in her eye.

That lady returned from the May Fayre having enjoyed herelf more than she had done for years. It had all been such *fun!* And of a kind she had never really indulged in. She had eaten ice-cream and toffee-apple and candy-floss, won a china duck at the hoopla stall which Jeremy eyed covetously so she gave it to him, as well as a coconut at the coconut shy. She could not remember when she had felt so light-hearted and – in the old-fashioned sense of the word – gay. Piers could never have brought himself to drive a dodgem, or ride a roundabout. He would have been stiff with embarrassment, called them childish. But James had never once seemed childish. He had entered into the spirit of things in a way which, she now realised, had encouraged her own self to break free of the constraints that time, habit and an always circumspect ten years with Piers had placed on it. Whatever else she might dislike about him, she had to admit that James Alexander had the most marvellous sense of humour, as well as an acute appreciation of the ridiculous. Piers' sense of humour was the kind that only ever saw jokes by appointment.

Which thoughts at once made her feel guiltily disloyal. Piers had other qualities. He was honest and steadfast and loyal and – dull, she thought. Face it, Harriet. Piers has all the life of a dead sparkplug. With horror she realised that before the advent of James Alexander she would not have given such a traitorous thought houseroom. But then, it was since his advent that the invasion had started.

That evening, there was a May Dance in the Church Hall, also in aid of the restoration fund, to which Harriet contributed fifty pounds. In the same blaze of recklessness she donned her froth of sea-green ruffles, only to be astonished at the transformation they brought about. For a start, the colour suited her no end, its boat shaped neckline showing off the line of her throat and its froth of skirts foaming about her like an incoming tide. The result was that she looked younger, prettier and much, much softer. Jeremy, who had been allowed to stay up and see the finery, put it nicely when he eyed her before saying limpidly: "Harriet, you look like a princess."

She dropped a kiss on his upturned face. "Why aren't you thirty years older?"

"I am," James Alexander offered helpfully. She ignored him.

She was never off the dance-floor for a minute. Normally she did not dance very often, had only learned because it was a skill needed in the social life her work brought her. Piers did not dance; he had two left feet, but Harriet did it well and she found it blissful to be whirled around the floor by someone who also knew what he was doing. Such as Charles, who for a big man was very light on his feet – and hers. It was such fun to dance the Valeta and the Palais Glide and the St Bernard Waltz, things she had never done before because her mother's warnings had turned her off going where she would encounter the opposite sex, and when, during a Paul Jones, she came face to face with James she was feeling charitable enough to smile at him nicely.

"Quite the belle of the ball," he commented, as he whirled her onto the floor.

"I'm having such a good time."

"I'd noticed."

Impulsively: "Thank you for bringing me this weekend."

"Changed your mind, then – about going to hell rather than anywhere with me?"

Her chin tilted "That was said under—"

"—duress?"

"Provocation."

"Then let's call it quits. If I provoked you, I apologise, but I have to tell you that it was in no way as provoking as you in that lovely dress. You look like Ondine."

Careful, Harriet warned herself. Remember Bert's warning. More mileage than a vintage Rolls. Plus when it comes to saying the right thing he's got more experience than a ventriloquist. Nevertheless she still felt a definite spurt of pleasure at the compliment besides which, he danced like a dream. Her doubts were waggling their fingers at her but she ignored them. Just for once, she thought, let me enjoy myself . . .

The festivities ended at midnight, but they lingered over a nightcap and a rehash of the day once back at Fairlawns and it was two a.m. by the time Harriet floated up to bed. Whether it was that last glass of champagne or the cumulative effect of her wonderful day she was not sure, but its power was such that it prompted her to say to James Alexander, who had accompanied her to her door: "Shall we bury the hatchet and shake hands?"

He took the hand she proffered and looking down at her consideringly held it for a moment before chiding: "Come now, Harriet, you can do better than that . . ." and tilting her chin, kissed her in a way that robbed her of all common sense. "Oh, yes . . . very much better," he murmured, lifting his head fractionally before pulling her tightly against his long length, where he proceeded to kiss the life out of her.

Harriet took the big fall. Piers had never kissed her like this. Nobody had ever kissed her like this. She had not known it was possible for a kiss to be like this. Why had she never understood what a *real* kiss was? It was doing for her as it went on and on, and she went with it willingly, all the way.

When at last he raised his head Harriet could not have moved to save her life. All she could do was hang on to those Oxford-blue eyes, noting bemusedly that they had gone very, very blue indeed. Still holding her eyes, he ended the embrace, reaching behind her to open her bedroom door.

"Goodnight, Harriet," he said, an odd note in his voice, before pushing her through the open door and closing it on her.

For a long time Harriet sat on the edge of her bed, staring at nothing. Then she got up and began to undress, moving like an automaton. She hung her dress away, cleaned her face, scrubbed her teeth, donned her nightdress, got into her comfortable bed and lay on her back for a few moments. He kissed me, she thought incredulously, feeling her stomach go into free fall, causing her to turn violently over and roll into a tight ball, where she huddled, trembling uncontrollably, since she now knew she could no longer evade the truth about just what it was that had raised her hackles so violently that first time she and James had met. She had been instantly and deeply attracted to him. Her instincts had sat up and begged but her mind – that powerful controller of all she was – had at once thrown the lever to switch the points that would shunt the attraction safely into the sheds of dislike. Except that for the first time ever the signals had failed.

Forcing herself to breath deeply and calmly she turned onto her back. It won't do, she reasoned. It will not do at all. He is out of my league. As Bert pointed out, I am most certainly not his usual class of bird, added to which haven't I always given cages a wide berth? Not to mention the fact that his aviary is at present presided over by a Bird of Paradise named Rina Cunningham. You would end up with your wings clipped. And you a high flier . . . No Harriet. Not this one. What do you want with the very thing your mother warned and warned you to avoid. An accomplished womaniser. You would never know a moment's peace; never know when he would stop the Rolls and turf you out onto a lonely road miles from anywhere. Best to back off before he backs you into corner. No, she told herself firmly. You have no choice. It still has to be 'Head Rules, OK'?

She was lying awake next morning after a night during which she had slept only fitfully, when she heard the sound of horses, and going to the window she saw

Corinne, mounted on a raking chestnut, followed by James on a satanic-looking black, walking their horses up the drive. Turning to the clock she saw it was seven forty-five. Too early to get up. On Sundays, she had been told, breakfast was not until ten a.m.

She was lying there, far out on the sea of her thoughts, when she heard her door open and sitting up she saw Jeremy's bright blond head appear round the door.

"Oh, good, you are awake," he said, coming in. "I've come to see if you would like to come and see Buttons now." He had obviously just woken up for he was still in his striped pyjamas.

"Yes, I would." Anything was better than lying here with her mind stuck in the groove of James Alexander.

"You had better get up and dressed, then."

"What about you? Is Nanny up?"

"I can dress myself now," he replied indignantly.

"I am sure you can," Harriet made hasty amends. "Give me five minutes, then come back for me."

She quickly splashed her face and put on a pair of Calvin Klein chinos and a pale blue shirt under a matching sweater. She was brushing her hair when Jeremy returned, his own shirt on inside out (but she knew better than to mention it) to say: "Come on then," before taking her by the hand.

Buttons was in the paddock behind the kitchen garden, grazing peacefully. He raised his head as Jeremy opened the gate, whinnied in recognition then came trotting across. He was a Shetland; broadbacked and the colour of mud, with a long mane and an even longer tail.

"Isn't he beautiful?" Jeremy asked proudly. "He is

four years old – younger than me, and I can ride him without a saddle. Shall I show you?"

"Are you allowed?"

"Oh, yes, I do it all the time. You'll have to lift me up, though."

Astride the Shetland's broad back, clutching handfuls of mane, Jeremy looked as completely at home on a horse as did his mother, and though Harriet was alarmed when he urged Buttons into a rapid trot it was soon obvious he was in no danger of falling off. They were all riders around here.

Unbidden, Harriet's mind pictured James Alexander in breeches and shirt, hands in string gloves, straight-backed and easy in the saddle, his hair blowing in the early-morning breeze, and from there it was a slow dissolve to a re-run of him kissing her and another free fall in space. 'All very fine', sneered her demon, 'but how many other women has he kissed that way – as a preliminary to taking them to bed? With his trade-in it must be a hell of a lot. How many of them has he brought here? Quite a few from what Corinne said. She assumed you were the latest, didn't she? He is so skilled at it he moves into action by pure reflex. A man like that would not take such a little thing as a kiss seriously so neither should you. Besides, he is holding a watching brief for Piers, never forget that, so it behoves you to be very circumspect around him. A kiss is one thing; just don't, let him take it any further.'

Attuned as he was, even at the age of six, Jeremy gazed thoughtfully at her taut face before sliding down from Buttons to take her hand and say: "Now I shall take you to see Banty."

"And who is he?"

114

"Not he, she. Banty is my hen. She's a Bantam so we call her Banty for short. She shares the paddock with Buttons but sometimes she goes into the kitchen garden to look for worms. Come on . . ."

Banty was in the midst of raspberry canes that were already heavily laden, and when Jeremy called her name came straight towards them in her high-stepping, imperious, bright-eyed way. Harriet bent down interestedly even as Jeremy warned: "I wouldn't do that if I were you—" and before the words had left his lips the hen had flown straight up into Harriet's face and pecked her savagely on her upper lip. It hurt like hell and blood spurted, mingling with the tears of pain which streamed from her eyes.

"Ouch!" She leapt backwards and upwards, hand to mouth.

"Oh, Harriet . . ." Jeremy let out a howl of terror and ran, shouting at the top of his voice: "Nanny . . . Nanny . . . Banty has pecked Harriet and she is all bleeding . . ."

James was in the stable yard unsaddling his horse when he heard Jeremy's terrified shouting, and tossing a quick: "See to Devil, will you," to a nearby groom, ran at once in the direction of the noise, meeting Jeremy as he pelted out of the kitchen garden, scooping him up in his long arms to ask: "All right, my lad, what's all the shouting about?"

"It's Banty . . . she has pecked Harriet and she is all blood—"

"Where is she?"

"In the kitchen garden . . . she bent down and Banty flew in her face and pecked her . . . I tried to tell her she shouldn't . . ."

"That damned hen will make a casserole yet," James warned, as he put Jeremy back on the ground. "Go on then, scoot to Nanny and tell her to get out the first-aid box. I'll bring Harriet."

Harriet's eyes were watering profusely because the pain was acute. The sharp beak had bitten cleanly into the sensitive flesh of her upper lip just beneath her nose. Her mixture of blood and tears had soaked her handkerchief but she was still vainly trying to stop the flow so as to be able to see when she heard someone say: "Good God, you look like you've had the worst of fifteen rounds with Mike Tyson. Let's have a look at the damage . . ."

She felt her chin taken in a firm but gentle hand and a fresh, dry handkerchief mop her up, first the blood then the tears, then back to the mouth again. She kept her eyes closed but she could feel him, like a flame.

"A nasty gash, deep but clean. I don't think you will need stitches. Jeremy should never have taken you to see that anti-social bird – unless, of course, Banty was only demonstrating her affection. You do have a tendency to provoke kisses, Harriet."

Harriet kept her eyes closed because she knew the teasing quality in his voice would be reflected in his face and eyes and was not up to facing either in her present emotional state of confusion. She felt him put his handkerchief into her hands and burying her face in it managed to rally and say: "If that is a demonstration of affection I'd rather have the will than the deed – ouch!" She winced because it hurt to speak.

"Stick to me," James advised. "I have never been

known to draw blood. Come on, let's go where I can administer some first aid."

Nanny was in the kitchen with Mrs Moody, the Herveys' cook, and on the wooden table between them was a big box with the red cross on it. Both women, of an age, clucked their tongues when they saw Harriet. "That dratted bird!" Nanny exclaimed. "Master Jeremy should have warned you."

"He did," Harriet said, wincing, "but Banty was too fast for him."

James sat Harriet on one of the kitchen chairs where she watched him pour TCP into the small china bowl of warm water Nanny handed him. Soaking a clump of cotton wool he tenderly wiped away the still welling blood then, with a, "Bite on the bullet, Harriet, I am now going to apply this neat," he applied a soaked cotton bud to the cut. Harriet's eyes watered again as it stung, but she held still, having no choice but to look up into the inky eyes only inches from hers. "Your lashes are all tangled," he said inconsequently, "but if you will wear fringes . . ." With deft gentleness he applied a piece of sterilised paper tape to the wound. "That will do for now, but it might be as well to have a doctor look at it just in case it needs a stitch."

Mrs Moody set before her a cup of freshly made tea, just as Jeremy sidled through the door, looking very hang-dog.

Holding out a hand Harriet said to him cheerfully: "It is just a little cut which looked far worse than it actually is."

"You are not cross with me? I should have told you Banty doesn't like strangers."

117

"Then by all means do so before you take anyone else to see her," Harriet suggested cordially.

"Oh, I will . . . honestly I will."

"If he doesn't he'll find himself eating chicken fricasee," warned James, washing his hands at the sink.

"You wouldn't do that, Uncle James. I know you wouldn't," Jeremy said confidently.

"Don't be too sure. I prefer my lady friends un-scarred, than you very much."

"Is Harriet your lady friend?"

"*A* lady friend," Harriet corrected, beginning as she meant to go on.

"Oh, Uncle James has lots of them."

"I know," Harriet said.

She had to drink her tea through a straw, and it was as she was doing so that the Herveys came into the kitchen, alerted by Nanny. They were both horrified, but Harriet would not hear of them punishing their son. "It was not really his fault, and he has had enough of a fright already."

"I only hope Piers won't think you've been roughly handled this weekend," Charles joked.

"Not for a moment," Harriet assured him. "He knows I can look after myself."

Over a gingerly eaten breakfast – not the bacon, eggs, tomatoes, mushrooms and kidneys the others put away but a boiled egg and soldiers, like the children, for they breakfasted with their parents on Sundays, she asked Corinne if she could take another look at the new house before returning to London that afternoon. In the course of her sleepless night she had come up with a few ideas.

"Of course. Charles shall drive you over."

But it was James at the wheel of his Jaguar she found waiting. "An urgent phone call for Charles, I am afraid," he said blandly. "I am to deputise – something I am rather good at, if you remember."

Just then Jeremy came hurtling out of the front door. "Mummy says I can come with you if you say I can."

"Of course," Harriet told him relievedly. "You can sit on my knee . . ."

"Coward," she could have sworn James said in a voice too low for Jeremy to hear, as he put the car in gear.

At the new house Harriet gave Jeremy her notebook and pencil to hold. "You can be my assistant."

As if taking the hint James said: "I'll leave you both to it then, and go and soak up some of this lovely sun. Give me a shout when you are ready to go back."

Harriet felt irrationally disappointed as she watched him saunter out. It was not until they got upstairs that on looking out of a window she saw him stretched out on the low wall bordering the terrace, hands clasped behind his head, eyes closed. Her instinct was to linger, drink her fill of him, so she moved away and got on with her work.

She was not sure when she missed Jeremy. She only knew she looked round after jotting down a rough sketch and he was not there. Retracing her steps through the house she could not find him so called his name, thinking he was playing a game of hide and seek. This house was full of cupboards, nooks and crannies; perfect hiding places all, but when she had checked every one of them he was still missing. Opening a window she called down to James to ask if he had seen him.

"No . . . he's probably lurking in ambush somewhere. You do the top floors again, I'll do the lower."

He was not on either.

"Right, I'll go and search the gardens." James said. "You see if there are any cupboards we might have missed."

The only thing she came across that she was sure she had not seen before was an iron-barred door at the end of a corridor which opened off the kitchen. Opening it she saw a flight of stairs leading down into darkness. Obviously a cellar and the last place a six-year-old would hide. Just in case she felt for the light switch, but when she clicked it there was no more than a flicker of electricity before it went dark again. Either the bulb had gone or the fuse had blown. Damn! Holding the door open with one hand she called loudly: "Jeremy . . . if you are down there come out, there's a good boy."

Silence. Then she thought she heard a noise like a stifled giggle.

"Jeremy! Come along now, this is no longer a joke . . ." Obviously he was not afraid of the dark. Annoyed now, because she was, she took her hand from the door and went inside to stand on the top step. "We are leaving now so you had better come up this instant . . ."

Silence. Then suddenly, total darkness. On unthinkingly taking her hand from the heavy door it had silently swung to closing behind her with a soft thud, striking her shoulder as it did so, knocking her off

120

balance and sending her sprawling. Clawing frantically at the stone wall she missed it as she fell, smacking her head on the handrail of the wooden bannister. By the time she hit the bottom she was out cold.

Eight

When she came round, the darkness pressed down on her like a ton weight. Sitting up gingerly she rubbed her sore head. Her shoulder hurt where she had banged it on a wooden stair, so did her shins, but when she carefully got to her feet nothing seemed to be broken.

Harriet Hilliard you are an idiot! she scolded herself. What on earth made you think a six-year-old would play hide and seek in a cellar? James Alexander seems to have done for every ounce of your common sense. Hanging on to the wooden rails for guidance as well as support she painfully climbed back up the stairs and feeling for the door pulled at the handle. It did not budge. She pulled hard, causing her shoulder to protest vigorously. There had been no key in the lock on the other side, she was sure of that, so it had to be stuck, probably swollen with age. This is all I need! she thought, feeling panic build. Balling her fists, which hurt as she did so, she banged on the door, shouting for help.

When, panting, she stopped to listen, pressing her ear against the door, the silence was total, like being muffled in black velvet. Her panic took a giant step forward. She did not like confined spaces, especially when there was no light; a legacy of her mother's method of punishment when Harriet was naughty: banishment to the cupboard under the stairs. That memory had her hammering the door again until her fists were sore, shouting all the time. Why did they not hear her? Then she remembered that the door was a thick one and that it was not in the kitchen but off it, at least forty feet down a passage. She had missed it herself the first time. Oh, God, she thought. Forcing calm she took several deep deep breaths and told herself to get a grip. James was not her mother, impervious to cries and pleadings. She only had to wait. Once he had found Jeremy they would both begin to look for her. She had no idea how long she had been shut in; the darkness was too total to see her watch, but it could not have been more than minutes. Minutes that felt like hours. She was preparing to bang and shout again when she heard the noise that had drawn her into the cellar into the first place, and it was a scuffle not a giggle, a skittering of feet. It had not been Jeremy – what in God's name had made her think it was Jeremy? It was rats! Weren't there always rats in cellars! That thought had her banging, kicking and shouting until suddenly the door was pulled open and she fell forward into strong, hard arms. She heard a sharply drawn breath: "In God's name, Harriet . . . what has happened to you?"

"I got shut in that damned cellar, that's what! The door swung to and knocked me flying. Didn't you hear me shouting?"

"Not until I came into the kitchen. This is one very thick door."

"You are telling me!" She felt an unaccountable urge to burst into tears.

124

"You seem to have banged yourself about some-what. This is just not your day, is it?"

"Of course I got banged! I fell down the cellar stairs. I hit my head and shoulder and my shins are probably red raw . . ."

She put up a hand to brush her hair from her eyes and left a smear of blood across her forehead. Siezing her palms James examined them before exclaiming: "Oh, my poor Harriet. But what on earth made you think Jeremy would hide in a dark cellar, much less manage to open a heavy door like this?"

"Because I couldn't find him anywhere else and I thought I heard him only it was rats and then the door swung behind me—"

"Because you did not latch it – see." He showed her the staple attached to the wall and the peg on its chain hanging on the inside of the door.

"How was I to know there was a latch?" Harriet flung at him. "All I was thinking of was Jeremy. Where is he anyway?"

"Outside. He'd gone wandering in the woods behind the house. I've had a few salutory words with him but the sight of you will frighten him to death!"

Harriet looked down at herself. Her chinos and shirt were dark with dirt. No doubt her face was the same. "How would you look if you had just fallen down a flight of steps?" she demanded, hearing her voice wobble. "I hammered on that damned door for ages . . . I thought you would never come!" And to her everlasting shame she burst into tears.

"Harriet . . . Harriet . . ." His voice soothed her like a balm. For the second time he wrapped her in his arms, putting her head against his shoulder. She could feel his strong fingers through her hair, comforting to such an extreme that it completely undid her, causing her to burst into a storm of weeping that had more to do with her emotional turmoil than her shock and injuries. Tears were a luxury to Harriet; in the protection of James Alexander's arms she revelled in that luxury to the hilt.

"Poor Harriet," he said, and this time he was not teasing. There was a sombre note to his voice. "Best get you back home. There is no water in the house yet but there's a bird-bath in the garden. I'll see if it is clean enough . . ."

Swinging her off her feet he carried her into the kitchen where he sat her on a draining board, giving her his handkerchief to dry her tears while he un-knotted the cravat from around his brown throat and took it outside. When he returned he said he had soaked it in rain water that had collected in a stone trough. Then, for the second time he proceeded, with achingly gentle tenderness, to clean first her her face, mindful of the injured lip, then her scraped hands, the frown on his face spurring Harriet to explain her tears.

"I hate confined spaces," she said miserably. "I suppose it is a childhood phobia. "My mother did not believe in physical punishment but she used to put me in the cupboard under the stairs when I misbe-haved."

"My phobia is crowds . . . I got lost in one of them once, separated from my own mother; it terrified the life out of me and even nowadays I tend to avoid them when I can. There – that's the best I can do for now.

When we get back I think a doctor ought to take a look at you in case you are concussed. You are not seeing double or anything?"

"No, but my head aches."

"You've got a nasty bruise just above your left temple." Shaking his head: "Piers is most definitely going to think you've been roughly handled this weekend. Probably won't ever let you go anywhere with me again." He sounded regretful but Harriet knew his tongue was embedded in his cheek. "Any more damage?" he queried.

"I banged my shoulder when I fell, that's all."

"Let's have a look-see." Turning her round he probed her back with those long, strong fingers.

"Ouch!"

"Hurts?"

"Tender," she lied. It was her susceptibilities that were giving her trouble.

"Well, you have no broken bones but I am afraid you are going to develop some lovely bruises. Just as well you were wearing trousers." Tongue in cheek: "But you always wear them, don't you."

Harriet opened her mouth to blast him only to lose her breath as he swung her up into his arms. "I can walk!"

"Relax; it will all be over in a minute."

When Jeremy, who had been lurking nervously, saw Harriet being carried he ran forward in tearful alarm. "Harriet . . . oh, Harriet . . . you are all hurt again . . ."

"All because of you," James said sternly. "In future, if you wish to wander off then kindly remember to tell somebody where you are going."

Jeremy's eyes welled. "I'm sorry," he quavered. "I just wanted to play in the garden."

"Which you are perfectly free to do – once somebody knows that you are doing so. Now, open the car door, there's a good boy."

Charles and Corinne were appalled when they saw her. "I don't know what to say, Harriet," Corrine confessed helplessly, "except that this weekend seems to have a hex on it."

Jeremy was sent to bed in disgrace despite Harriet's protests that the true cause was her own stupidity, not being familiar with the ways of children. She made no mention of the real reason. As it was he took charge of the situation, insisting on carrying her upstairs to her bedroom, where he deposited her carefully on her bed while he ran her a hot bath. In the bathroom mirror she got her first sight of her ruined face. Her right cheekbone was a mass of scratches on a bed of lilac bruising; she had another large bruise on one temple and what with the sticking plaster on her lip she looked for all the world like a battered wife.

While she soaked, Corinne went to call her doctor.

He said there were no bones broken, nor was she concussed, just banged up; no need for a stitch in her lip as the cut was small though deep, but twenty-four hours in bed woud not come amiss. He re-cleaned her cuts with antiseptic, administered a tetanus injection 'just in case' and gave her a sedative, after which she slept until seven o'clock, waking to find herself stiff and sore but able to drink a welcome cup of tea and receive a penitent Jeremy.

"Please don't be angry with me," he pleaded, lower lip trembling.

"I am not, but I would like you not to do a disappearing act with anyone else."

"Oh, I won't, I've already promised Mummy and Daddy and Uncle James too . . . He was very cross with me. I won't ever do it again, honest."

"That's my good boy."

More cheerfully: "Would you like me to sit with you for a while? We could play Snakes and Ladders."

"While you play on Harriet's sympathy? No way," said James from the doorway. "Nanny is looking for you, my lad, with a sponge. You can come and see Harriet again tomorrow."

"Kiss me good-night, then," Harriet requested, proffering her cheek. He added a hug for good measure.

When he had gone: "I have persuaded Piers not to come down post-haste," James said without preamble. "I told him you need forty-eight hours rest and that Corinne and Charles are only too happy to see that you get it. He was all for sending his own ambulance. I'll call the shop tomorrow and say you, won't be in for a couple of days."

"I am not at death's door!"

"No, but you had a nasty shock. Why else would you, of all women, dissolve into tears?" Then he smiled. "But I now know what to do with you when you get stroppy. Lock you in the broom cupboard."

"That will be the day!"

His smile became a laugh. "That's more like it. I can see your spirit level rising." Without so much as a by-your-leave he sat down on the bed. "Cheer up," he counselled. "I am sure you will make a most impatient invalid but you are stuck with it so put a brave face on it. It is one, after all."

He took her chin between finger and thumb, turned her face this way and that. "Another two inches and you would have had a beautiful shiner," he observed dispassionately. "And it is just as well you don't intend to have your palm read . . . plus two broken fingernails. All in all, not your usual dauntingly elegant self – though infinitely more approachable."

"I haven't noticed you keeping your distance." It was out before she could stop it.

His slow smile was pure wickedness. "I was never one to resist a challenge."

Their eyes met and Harriet's anger swirled away as her stomach went down the drain, but he laid down her hands and stood up. "Now then, orders are that after supper you are to take one of these little red pills the doctor left, in order to ensure a good night's sleep, and I am also under Piers' orders, which are to see that you receive the best of care and attention. Is there anything else you want?"

"No, thank you."

"Then I will bid you a very good night."

But it was not. After some fluffy scrambed egg on two slices of thick buttered toast she read for a while before taking her pill and switching off her lamp. Only to fall into a nightmare.

She was back in the cellar, but this time she was bound hand and foot and the rats were scurrying all over her. She could feel their sharp feet, see their red eyes, feel their whiskers, hear their squeaks, but all under the furious denunciation of her mother's voice. 'I told you, didn't I? Never trust a man. They all practice emotional enslavement. Now look where you have landed yourself! In the very jail I warned you to avoid at all costs'.

Harriet opened her mouth to deny everything but nothing came out. When she tried to speak she could not, nor could she scream, try though she might. And then she felt two hands come out of the darkness and take hold of her, whereupon she went wild, thrashing about in an effort to free herself until quite suddenly she was free, coming out of her terror at the same time to find herself on her knees in the bed, her body damp with sweat and entangled in the sheets, heart cantering, breath whistling, frantically clutching the lapels of James Alexander's dark red silk dressing gown.

"It's all right", he calmed. "You were having a nightmare."

Harriet drew in deep breaths, before saying on a shudder: "I dreamt I was back in the cellar with rats running all over me—"

"Delayed reaction."

"Was I making lot of noise?"

"Enough to wake me – but I sleep like a cat."

"I'm sorry to have disturbed you . . . it was all so horribly real . . ."

"Nightmares usually are." Smoothing her damp, tangled hair back from her face: "You are soaked. Have you another nightgown?"

"In the top drawer of that chest."

"You go and put it on then, and I'll see to the bed."

She managed to turn on the shower in spite of her taped hands and stand under it for a soothing five minutes, feeling clean and somewhat restored when she dropped the cool satin of a fresh nightgown over

131

her head. In the bathroom mirror, the inadvertent sight of her face made her wince and turn away.

Re-entering her bedroom she found that James had remade the bed with fresh linen, which felt wonderful as she slid into it.

"Sorry to be such a nuisance," she apologised not looking at him. "I'm not usually so—"

"Human? Have I complained?"

"No, but—"

"Harriet, even machines break down, and in spite of your efforts to run your life like one there will always be the human factor, thank God."

Harriet kept her eyes on her hands, unconsciously plucking at their plaster, somewhat damp from the shower.

"Don't do that, there's a good girl," he said, sitting down on the bed and possessing himself of them. Harriet stared down at his own hands and the small jagged scar at the base of the middle finger on his right hand.

"Are you all right now? Demons all gone?"

She nodded.

"Do you want another pill?"

She shook her head.

"Does it hurt your mouth to speak?"

Another shake of the head.

"That's all right then," he said, and kissed her. It was meant to be comforting, reassuring, but shouldering her cool head aside her heated emotions took over, opening her mouth under his in a way that had him pressing her back against the pillows, his body urgent against hers as they kissed each other in a way that had all coherent thought left for dead in seconds. Harriet was conscious only of his mouth and tongue and the havoc they were playing with her reason, which was screaming blue murder and hammering on the bars of its cage. In a display of electrifying passion she abandoned her scruples along with all control in a way that was met and matched by James Alexander. Never had she lost herself this way with Piers because he was incapable of provoking such a response, since he appeared to have learned about sex from manuals. James Alexander, on the other hand, had been born knowing it. When his mouth left hers to trail fire down her throat and her breasts once his hands had pushed her nightgown away from her shoulders, Harriet found herself arching to it, and when he she felt it envelop a fondant pink nipple, his tongue flicking, teeth nipping, she made a sound such as she had never made, causing James to apply the brakes. He lifted his mouth, drawing up and away so as to look into her eyes. His own were as blue as a pool of ink, lit from beneath. She could see her own flushed face reflected in them.

Silently they looked deep into each other. A little pulse fluttered at the side of Harriet's mouth, which felt all bruised and pulpy. His own face was wiped clean. No way of telling what he was thinking or feeling. But his actions were decisive when he put her arms inside the covers before reaching out a hand to switch off the lamp. She felt him get up off the bed, heard her bedroom door open then close. He was gone.

And so was she. All of a sudden Harriet Hilliard, who had always known where she was going, was in country totally unknown to her, without a single familiar landmark or anything in the way of a pointer as to the right direction to take. And she knew why. The heartless womaniser she could have contended with – and won. It was what she now knew lay behind the sexual charisma: kindness, for instance, allied to a tenderness and caring that had her sense of direction all shot to hell. Just as she knew that as yet, she had not even begun to plumb his depths . . .

She was pale and heavy-eyed next morning, causing Corinne to insist she stay in bed. "I don't like the look of you at all. Are you in pain?"

"No," lied Harriet, her tumble-dried emotions stiff and sore.

"Probably the after-effects of yesterday . . ." Corinne paused then asked, prompted by the pale face, the haunted-looking eyes. "Is anything wrong?"

Harriet met the concerned gaze. You've been there. she thought. You could tell me the best thing to do, but even as she framed the thought she knew she would never ask. She had been brought up not to. "No," she lied again. "It's the after-effects, that's all."

The first thing she did when Corinne had closed the door behind her was reach for the phone by her bed and call Piers. "I want you to come and fetch me."

"Of course I will, darling. Right away. If I leave now I can be there in a couple of hours. Are you badly hurt?"

"Just cuts and bruises, but I'll do better at home. Corrine is kindness itself but you know me, I like my own surroundings." Where she could sit down and think her way out of this impossible situation.

Corinne wasn't convinced: "Are you sure? You are welcome to stay here as long as you like, you know."

"You are very kind, but I have imposed upon you long enough."

"But I feel this is all our fault . . ."

"No. I brought everything on myself." And how! she thought. "I still intend to do your house; just let me get myself together and in a few days I'll be as right as rain and raring to go."

Corinne had recognised a strong will from the start so did not press the issue, nor did she ask why Harriet had gone to the trouble of making Piers come and collect her when she knew James would have driven her back to town. Something Had Occurred. James had been somewhat distraught, had left the house early to go riding. Corinne's king-sized curiosity was eating her out of house and home, but she knew there would be no satisfaction to be obtained from Harriet, who had once more gone behind the stainless steel of her public persona. What had happened to the gay, light-hearted, even frivolous girl who had ridden the roundabouts and danced the night away? Obviously, she decided, James had made a pass which Harriet had intecepted and returned. Which again was not the norm. James was not one to fumble at anything where a woman was concerned. He had too much experience. Her match-making instincts had taken fire when she saw them together, ignited by the sparks they so obviously struck. So why then had the fire gone out – or been put out, she corrected herself? By a bucketful of Harriet's ice-water? In God's name Harriet, why? she longed to ask. Surely you cannot prefer a sheep like Piers Cayzer to a lion like James?

"I don't understand it," she complained to her

husband later. "I was sure something was going on between them."

"You mean you hoped it was. You will read things into situations on which nothing has been written! Didn't I warn you not to meddle?"

"But I didn't meddle, as such. I just – put them in each other's way."

"Then somebody obviously tripped and fell flat on their face – probably Harriet. I have never known James to stumble."

Which had Corinne frowning and biting her lip. "I wonder . . ."

Harriet kept to her room until Piers arrived. He was upset by what he termed 'her poor face', and proceeded to fuss and cluck until she wanted to scream, but he was her lifeline out of the abyss over which she felt she was suspended, so she went along with it. All she wanted to do was get away.

"Where's old James, then?" Piers asked, eventually, surprised at not seeing him.

"Riding," Corinne told him.

"Oh, well . . . I suppose he could do no more than he has done. It is as well he was on the spot; always a good man to have in a crisis, is James – and Charles too, of course," he added hastily, mindful of the man whose fag he was at Eton.

"It was not a crisis," Harriet corrected from between clenched teeth. "Only a stupid accident which I brought on myself. Charles and Corinne have been marvellous."

"Two accidents," corrected Piers pedantically. "First that hen and then the cellar—"

"Piers, we already feel bad enough . . ." Corinne

136

protested. "My youngest son has gone into hiding."

But he appeared as Piers solicitously helped Harriet into his Rolls, very hang-dog. "I'm truly sorry, Harriet," he whispered, eyes welling. "I didn't mean you to be hurt."

"I am sorry too – to have to leave you. But we will see each other a lot when I come down to do your new house, won't we?" He brightened with relief, confidence returning, giving her a heartfelt hug and a big kiss – on the cheek so as not to hurt her lip – but he did not look at Piers. He hid behind his mother's skirt instead.

Harriet was beginning to relax as it seemed she would be able to get away without having to face James, but just then the big black horse came trotting down the drive. Piers was out of the car in an instant, wringing James' hand as well as ringing the peal of his thanks. Finally, with a last goodbye he got into the car again and Harriet silently urged him to get going. Which was when James put his head through the open window to say: "Goodbye, Harriet. I am sure your wounds will leave no scars."

Harriet met the onslaught of those all-seeing eyes head on. "I heal quickly," she told him ringingly.

They were on the M4 almost into London when she said: "I've been thinking. There really is no need for James to come into the shop any more. The Harcourt-Smith job is finally over and done with and once I am over this little – *contretemps* – I can go back to managing on my own."

"Not to worry," Piers told her cheerfully. "He's off to Bermuda with Rina, didn't he tell you? Won't be

137

back for at least six weeks. Said to tell you it was short but very sweet besides which he knows you are a one-woman band used to playing your own tunes."

Only when Piers told her that James was no longer in England, did she feel secure enough to return to the shop, to be greeted by a general chorus of anxious enquiries as to her state of health and disappointment as to the departure of James Alexander.

"I shall miss him," Evelyn said wistfully. "He was such fun to have around – livened up the day no end."

Even Miss Judd expressed regret. "A pity." was her verdict. "He was nobody's fool, that one."

No, he just took me for one, Harriet thought. But she found she missed him as she had never missed anything or anyone in her life. Acutely and miserably and endlessly. She no longer got up in the morning filled with eager anticipation as to what the day would bring. She missed catching sight of him around the shop, of sitting with him discussing a colour scheme or the right pictures to compliment a setting; she missed their stimulating arguments, their verbal jousting, his wit, his verve. Most of all she missed the sheer physicality of the man himself.

So she plunged into the deep end of her pool of work, surfacing only to sleep or see Piers. She determined that Sheringham Court would be her crowning achievement. James Alexander would have no cause to regret his recommendation.

When she took her finished sketches down to the Herveys they were delighted. "Harriet, these are absolutely wonderful!" Corinne gloated. "James was so right about you . . . I can't wait for the work to start. When will it?"

"Next week, if that is all right with you?"

"Whenever you are ready . . . How long do you think it will take?"

"I should think eight to ten weeks."

"Good. James will be back by then – you know he is in Bermuda with Rina – so he can come to the house-warming – at which you, of course, will be the guest of honour."

Piers approved of her working for the Herveys. "Nice couple – though I think they might apply a little more discipline to their children. Especially the one that caused you so much trouble . . ."

"Piers, he is a child, and a charming one, added to which I was the one who caused the trouble, not him. He wandered off, that's all. Six-year-olds do that, you know."

"Do they?" Piers commented, in a voice that said his children wouldn't.

Harriet worked like a beaver through June and July, and the house was finished, as she had promised, by early August. Once the children were free of school for the summer, the Herveys had taken themselves off to Virginia to visit Corinne's parents, leaving Harriet to supervise the final removal from one house to the other. When everything was in place, every piece of furniture sited just so, every piece of crystal and porcelain displayed to best advantage, every picture hung in the perfect spot, Harriet made it her final job to fill Corrine's exquisite Chinese vases with fresh flowers. It would be a nice touch when they returned to take up residence the following day. So she ransacked the garden and greenhouse of the old house and took armfuls of radiant blooms across to the new one. The housewarming was planned for the following weekend, but she had already decided not to attend. The thought of seeing James Alexander with Rina Cunningham on his arm was pure self-flagelation, and Harriet was no masochist.

She had reached another milestone on her journey of self-discovery. That she could be jealous, if that was what the demonic agony she suffered could be termed. But her will was stronger. Long though she might to see that laughing, handsome face, look into those blue-black eyes which saw so deep even as they melted you down to a puddle with the power of his sexuality, she was still capable of refusing to accept what he offered because she knew – now – that she only had to drop the handkerchief and it would be in his hands before it hit the floor. The trouble was it would be on his terms, and she was still her mother's daughter, with eighteen years of conditioning controlling her actions at all times. Unconditional surrender was something she had been warned to avoid at all cost, and though, after a long hard day, sleep was still driven away by physical longing, she was not able to hold out her hands for his cuffs, to be taken into his custody for as long as *he* decided, which would calculatedly be long enough to render her his prisoner for life. No and no and NO!

She finished arranging the last two vases of flowers which she then took along to the master bedroom. It was the most beautiful room in the house, with a scrolled ceiling and a bank of windows occupying one wall. Harriet had decorated it in peony-pink and white, its specially made bed – eight by eight to accommodate Charles Hervey's heroic frame – covered in a toile of the same colours; matching the draped and swagged curtains, and the covers and cushions of the window seat. Her feet sank into the deep velvety pile of the woven plain carpet as she went across to place one vase on the lovely American early nineteenth century tallboy, an heirloom given to Corinne by her maternal grandmother, who had in turn inherited it from hers. The dressing table was a matching sofa table on which she had placed a standing mirror of the same period with twin candlesticks cleverly wired to burn electricity, and she placed her second vase of fat, pale pink and deep rose peonies there.

That done, she sank onto the stool in front of the dressing table – its seat one of Corrine's embroidery masterpieces – and stared at herself in the mirror. She looked tired, and every pound of the much needed weight she had gained had once more been lost, the bags under her eyes packed with nights of sleeplessness. She was right back to where she had been six months ago. Physically, that was. Emotionally she had travelled a long, hard way.

Through the mirror she stared at the big bed and for once let her mind wander, free of the constraints she nowadays placed on it, imagining what it would be like to be loved by James Alexander. She had only Piers to use as a valid comparison, but she now knew, after the brief foretaste he had given her, that it would be mind-bending, that he could give her pleasure the likes of which she had never so much as begun to comprehend. She envied Rina Cunningham with all her heart, but her mother's warnings, repeated on the hour, every hour, seven days a week, fifty-two weeks a year for the first eighteen years of her life kept her chained to her fears, added to which, most important of all she had given her word to Piers, and she had never welched on a deal in her life.

It was on getting back to town she found her IOU had been called in.

"Darling, dearest Harriet you will never guess! Paula has at last gone and filed suit for an uncontested divorce on the grounds of the irretrievable breakdown of our marriage! James called me from Bermuda – warned me what to expect – he saw her in Hamilton with her new man. According to the lawyers I should be free in six short weeks! Isn't that absolutely marvellous? I am so happy I could fly!" He broke off at the sight of her face. "Darling . . . forgive me . . . I should have broken it to you gently, but I am so absolutely cock-a-hoop. James warned me it would floor you. To tell you the truth, of late I have been expecting you to tell me you had had enough of all this waiting. You seemed so fed up . . . I know Paula agreed to a divorce but she did not seem to be doing anything about it. I was beginning to think it was another of her little games, that's why I confided in James. I knew he would do something to get things going again. I think we should have him as my best man, don't you? I know you don't particularly care for him, but for this once . . ."

Harriet closed her eyes, clenched her hands until her nails bit into her now healed palms. Why? she was screaming inwardly. Why has he done this? If he knows that it is the last thing I want why is he

142

force-feeding me with it? Is it a case of his guilty conscience, since he foisted Paula onto Piers in the first place? Or is he putting me in my place for daring to so much as think of him instead of Piers; punishing me for eyeing the temptation he dangled in front of me? I was right to back away. He doesn't give a damn about me. He was merely testing my feelings for Piers, who is his real concern. What he wants – what he has only ever wanted – is to make sure Piers is not short-changed a second time.

But deep down she was in mourning. How *could* he? And he said *I* was a fraud . . .

Nine

So she went to the housewarming. She would not give him the satisfaction of confirming his classification of her as a moral coward. She would show him what *she* believed in: honouring your word, meeting your obligations and accepting responsibility for your own actions. Most of all she would show him once and for all that she was not to be manipulated by such as him. But to confirm the rightness of her battle-plan she went up to see her mother first.

This time Mrs Hilliard knew her daughter at once, launching her usual hymn of praise and justification, which Harriet took unto herself and applied as a healing ointment to her badly bruised ego. They spent the morning together, had lunch and went for a stroll in the gardens, able to talk coherently for the first time in a long time without her mother slipping in and out of alternate dimensions, though she still conducted her war games. But when it was time for Harriet to leave, Mrs Hilliard put her arms about her daughter to say happily: "Oh, it does what is left of my heart good to see you so happy and successful, to know you have fulfilled my every dream. I am so proud of you, Harriet, for doing it my way." With a brimming look such as Harriet had never seen her mother finished simply: "You have redeemed my life . . ."

But what about *my* life, Mother? Harriet found herself asking as she drove back down the M1. What am I going to do about appetites you did not so much as mention. You told me to avoid on-the-make men, but not the feelings they can arouse. How do I deal with *them*? I never expected to find myself – what? she thought, shying away from the figure wearing the label 'Love' in the identity parade line-up. Powerfully and deeply sexually attracted, she substituted, Yes, that's it. Somehow he has managed to get to me as no other man ever has. I know he is a disastrous choice – except that I never actually got to choose – because one woman will never be enough for him, and I find that what I want is to be the only one.

Oh, well, she thought at the end of her journey as she turned into Park Lane, at least you are happy, Mother. I am glad somebody is.

Piers drove her into Gloucestershire late on the Saturday afternoon. They had been invited for the weekend, but so had James and Rina. Harriet at once therefore pleaded a meeting on the Friday and a long-standing client luncheon on the Saturday. She had no intention of spilling blood on Corinne's hideously expensive new carpet, therefore the less time she spent standing on it the better. A couple of hours, no more, should do it.

But that night, as soon as she set eyes on Rina, exhibiting her glorious body in tight white silk crepe, draped cunningly à la Madame Gres, she felt utterly quenched. Her own dress was a Belville Sassoon, drifts of pure silk chiffon which matched her eyes. She had chosen it deliberately because it concealed her loss of weight, being high at the throat and long at the sleeve, with a full skirt to conceal hip bones which now protruded like coat hangers. She had made up her face carefully, applying blusher like a defiant flag, and hung miniature diamond chandeliers in her ears, but she knew it was only a case of painting the sepulchre. Just so long as her badly cracked foundations held until this terrible evening was over.

After greeting Harriet, Corrine, her advanced state of pregnancy concealed under a caftan that emulated Joseph's Many-Coloured Dreamcoat, tucked her arm through that of 'her favourite designer' before proceeding to do a lap of honour, introducing her to all and sundry as 'the instigator of all this beauty, down to the last cache-pot'. Harriet moved through it all unseeingly, flesh-tinglingly conscious only of James Alexander, Rina at his side, standing at the far end of the long drawing room, which Harriet had done in varying shades of green, from jade to pistachio, to complement the white and gold Louis XVI furniture and sumptuous Aubusson carpet. Harriet had not seen him for many long weeks, every day of which she had counted off on her calendar.

As they approached, James smiled. "Well, Harriet. . ." She made herself stand under the shimmering eyes as they went over every inch of her, but all he said was: "Not a scar to be seen. You do indeed heal fast, but then, I ought to have remembered that it does not do to underestimate any of *your* capabilities. Congratulations, you have lived up to every one of my expectations." He then introduced her to Rina, who nodded with bored indifference, once a quick scan had seen there was no competition.

147

Glancing from James to Harriet and then back again, Corinne felt uneasy. On the surface the words were innocuous, but she knew James was applying the lash, while Harriet stood there as though she was counting every stroke. Piers, of course, only stood and beamed. How can you not *sense* it? Corinne raged at him silently. How come you are so hyper-acute to every shift in the money market yet as unfeeling as a bag of coins when it comes to people! Can't you see what is going on? Are you blind as well as deaf and dumb?

"I understand more congratulations are in order?" James was saying. "When is the happy day?"

"Six weeks time," Piers answered proudly.

"I look forward to receiving my invitation. I always go to Piers' weddings, you know," he added to Harriet, standing stiff as a stalagmite.

Corrine threw him a glare that would have slain a gorgon, before bearing Harriet away, but as she did so she heard Harriet say one word to James, so quietly she only just caught it. "Why?"

"Why not?" James responded, just as quietly, but it was a gauntlet flung. They moved on, then, but when Corinne looked back she saw that James was looking after them – or rather at Harriet. And he was frowning. As well you might, she fulminated. I shall have a few cogent words to say to you later!

When they had done their circuit, Corrine said: "One last VIP. My youngest son. He refuses to sleep until he sees you. Would you mind?"

Harriet's smile was her first, real one of the night. "It would be a pleasure."

"You know the way – you were the one who

148

suggested putting the nursery where it is. I am afraid I still have to play hostess."

Jeremy was sitting up in bed, all expectation, "I waited and waited," he reproached. "Why didn't you come when Uncle James did? I don't like that other lady he has brought. All she says to me is 'Run along, little boy' and I'm not little, I am nearly seven!"

"Of course you are not little," Harriet agreed indigantly.

"I asked Uncle James where you were and he said you were busy digging your own grave. You are not going to die, are you, Harriet? You were not really hurt when you fell down the stairs or when Banty bit you?"

"Of course not. Your Uncle James is a tormenting tease, you know that. Do I look as though I am dying?"

Jeremy smiled, and then said, as if he had known it all the time: "I knew Uncle James was teasing. He teases everybody."

"Yes. He teases me too."

"Are you a working lady tonight, Harriet? That dress does not make you look like a princess the way the other one did."

"Tonight I am indeed a working lady, come to see if everyone is pleased with what I did to your new house. Are you?"

"Nanny says she has room to spare and that's a good thing, and I like the big cupboard for my toys. James and I both have our own rooms now, you know."

"Yes," said Harriet. "I arranged it."

"Did you? Well I'm glad you did. James always used

to boss me around when we had to share. Now I can put my toys where I like."

They chatted amicably for about ten minutes then Nanny came in to say it was already way past Master Jeremy's bedtime, and once that was accomplished Harriet spent another ten minutes being congratulated on her sterling work. She was about to go dowstairs again when Corinne came looking for her.

"Piers is fretting," she explained with a 'you know how he is' look. "I don't think he trusts you with us any more."

"I was just telling Miss Hilliard that the house is lovely but she does not look too good herself. Worn to the bone if you ask me – and far too thin even if it is the fashion nowadays."

Corinne tactfully abstracted Harriet before Nanny could tread on any more badly worn toes, but as they went back down to the party trod carefully herself when she said delicately: "Look, Harriet, tell me to mind my own buiness if you like but – you and James – I thought—"

"Don't!" Harriet interrupted flatly in a KEEP OUT – THIS MEANS YOU voice. "I told you once before: I do not play in his league – or his game, for that matter."

That's all very well, Corinne thought, but just what is his game right now?

Piers was hovering and as soon as she had him alone: "Do you mind if we leave now?" Harriet asked. "I have a splitting headache."

"Of course." She could see he was just as pleased. Piers was not a party animal. Corrine did not protest, only kissed Harriet warmly, as did Charles.

"You will keep in touch, won't you? Just because the job is over it does not mean our friendship has to go the same way . . . and with the baby – which, by the way, my scan says is the girl we want – growing ever larger and more rumbunctious I don't get around so much any more."

"I will come and see you whenever I can," Harriet promised. But not when *he* is here, she added silently. After that skin-stripping encounter she had decided that a rational and realistic approach was the only one to take to this highly emotive issue. As well as the safest. A fat lot of good it had done her to let her imagination and expectations run loose. They had only coiled themselves around her heart and strangled her.

As the front door closed on them: "For girl about to be married, Harriet looks as as if she is about to be hanged," Charles commented on a frown.

"She *is* hanging," his wife told him shortly, "and right now I am going to say a few words to her executioner."

"Ah, Corinne," James greeted her with a smile when she went up to him. "Finished the lap of honour?"

"Yes. Harriet and Piers have just left so I can now regard my duty done and enjoy myself."

"Gone!" An expression too fleeting to identify flashed cross his face; chagrin, she decided, but also something else . . . Regret? Disappointment? What on earth are you playing at? she wondered crossly. You no more want Harriet to marry Piers Cayzer than I do, so why in God's name have you made it your business to bring it about?

"You have not yet danced with me," she reminded.

"Then let me remedy the omission at once." He

151

removed Rina's possessive hold on his arm. "Hang onto Charles," he advised, "he is great deal steadier than I am."

As they went into the room where the dancing was: "I don't think Harriet looked too good, did you?" Corinne cast her line. "Charles was just saying she looks like anything but a bride-to-be."

"Harriet knows what she's doing," James replied, non-committally.

"Ah, but does she? Piers is the last man I would have chosen for her."

"Harriet does her own chosing."

"Come off it, James, she is being pushed into this and you are the guy who is crowding her."

"Put it down to amends to make."

Corinne gave him a look so old-fashioned it was Victorian. "Where women are concerned you have no conscience, besides which I think we have both arrived at the same conclusion in our dealings with Harriet: she is the kind of woman who honours her obligations, and if Piers Cayzer is anything more to her than an obligation I'll eat the brand-new, hideously expensive Philip Treacy hat I have bought to wear at my daughter's christening!"

By now Corinne had the bit between her teeth. "That first accident-prone weekend you brought her down, I asked you how on earth Piers had managed to find such a pearl and I distinctly remember you saying that he hadn't but she had. What did you mean, because you also told me it was not his money she was after?"

"It wasn't and isn't."

"Than do tell. I want to help if I can, James. Harriet

is in trouble, and I like her too much to let her make what I am sure is a grievous mistake. I am positive that what she is doing is not what she wants to do. I tried to help but she cut me off at the ankles. Sometimes I think she carries that self-sufficiency of hers to ridiculous lengths."

James was silent again then he said abruptly: "It is my considered belief that Harriet only agreed to marry Piers because she was sure she would never be called upon actually to do so. But she did use him; as a means of keeping other men at bay. Nothing was ever actually *said* and it was all very discreet because of Piers and his paranoia, but everybody accepted that she was spoken for, and by whom. Piers was the smokescreen which allowed her to devote all her attention to what she really loved – loves: *Harriet Designs*. At some time in her life she has been brainwashed into believing that men are The Enemy and that any kind of emotional or economical dependence on them is death." He stopped dancing abruptly. "I feel in need of a drink. Let's go find one."

With a second glassful in his hand after downing the first at a gulp, James said: "Do you really want to help?"

"Indeed I do."

"Then let's talk." Taking her elbow he walked her into her sitting room, where Harriet had carefully bestowed the choicest items from the Hervey collection of porcelain. Shutting the door behind them he carefully helped Corinne to lower herself into the largest of her lovingly embroidered chairs before pulling up a long stool to face her.

"You were right about me pushing. I leaned on

Paula too. I told her that unless she agreed to a fast no-fault divorce I'd make known certain little – peccadil-loes – every one of which would crucify her socially and be the death of her ambitions. I even went so far as to introduce her to a man with more money than Piers but absolutely none of his scruples, who will lead her a hell of a dance and dose her daily with her own medicine. My reason was I hoped that if I forced the issue, shoved Harriet right up against the fact that she would actually have to become Mrs Piers Cayzer, she would realise that in the last analysis, she just could not do it."

"Thus leaving the field free for you?" asked Corinne shrewdly.

"It was a way of killing the proverbial two birds . . ." he admitted.

Corrine sat back. "Well . . ." she said, "you always were a devious piece of work, and some would say that your come uppance is long overdue, but I have to tell you that though I am very happy for you, I also never, ever thought to see the day."

"Snap," agreed James wryly.

Shaking her head in disbelief. "The biter bit," Corrine observed.

"Harriet is my own, personal Banty." Smiling with-out humour: "I had reached the age – and stage – where I accepted that I was never likely to come across that one particular woman who could make me break out in a cold sweat at the very thought of not spending the rest of my life with her. They came – and as you well know – they went."

"Like yo-yos," Corinne agreed.

"Harriet was – different. When Piers told me about

154

her and her situation and asked me to fill in while she took a break I thought she sounded like a Margaret Thatcher clone, and there are men who like to be told what to do by bossy women. However, the moment I met Harriet I knew that there was far, far more to her than had ever met Piers' short-sighted eyes. You know me; I am of a curious turn of mind and my tendency is to probe beneath surfaces that appear to have no depth. Sometimes they don't – Rina, for instance – but when they do – and Harriet is bottomless, by the way – my attention is well and truly caught. My first impression was that she was a control freak; as capable as they come and aggressively independent, but terrified to let go; hanging on like grim death when there was so much as the mere suggestion of it – like my taking over for six weeks. What also struck me as odd was why a woman as assertive as she was would be involved with a man as unassertive (except where money is concerned) as Piers Cayzer. So I decided I would take the job on and spend six weeks finding out. I had this strong gut feeling you see, that under the state-of-the-art casing there was an entirely different woman; moreover, one she would not allow herself to be; the one Piers would not know if she came up in the street and accosted him, because all he knows is her surface. With him she has never even begun to open up." Pause. "But she has with me, and it proved I was right about her." James shook his head. "The real Harriet Hilliard would scare Piers to death."

"But not you?"

"No . . . anything but. The real Harriet can light a fire such as a man could warm himself at for a life-time."

"Ah . . ." Corinne said, sounding satisfied. "I *knew* something had happened." Then: "And did you? Find out, I mean."

"What? Oh, yes . . . far more than I had bargained for. Trouble was, so did she."

Corinne looked at him enquiringly.

"I seemed to act like a computer virus," James explained. "One that sent *Harriet Designs* out of whack, thus allowing Harriet Hilliard to escape. The one has been trying to eradicate the other ever since and failing signally. You saw how she looked tonight."

"At first glance – and we know who is responsible, don't we?"

"I had no choice, Corinne. I know what I have done just as I know I had to do it. This is about me as well as Harriet and I am as selfish as the next man. I want – God, how I want – Harriet to get rid of both *alter ego* and Piers and admit what she really wants."

"Which is?"

"Me," James answered simply.

Corinne assimiliated that. "And she knows that you know all this?"

"Why do you think she is fighting so hard? Of course I saw the way she looked tonight and hated it as much as you do, but nor can I stand the thought of her going back to that Business Before Pleasure At All Times lifestyle; I want her to face up to and accept the facts *as they are* not the way she prefers them to be."

"Which are?" asked Corinne.

"That she sees losing her precious independence as some kind of betrayal; of what or whom I have yet to find out, which has everything to do with her intention to marry a man she does not love merely because she once told him she would."

Caught by his frustration Corinne reached out to touch his arm. "It hurts, doesn't it?"

Looking up he met her gaze. "Yes."

"So why on earth haven't you told her all this?"

"Because it has to be what *she* wants, of her own free will. Oh, I could have her body if I put my mind to it but it is Harriet's mind *and* body I want; Harriet *herself*; all that she is, all that she is not. I want her to admit that she wants me and is only too happy to come to me of her own free will, consciously and deliberately; more – glory in it and not be afraid – because that is what is behind it all; some terrible fear of commitment. What I don't yet know is why."

"Oh, dear," Corinne said, "you *are* in love . . . Mr No-Comitment himself."

"I have got to the stage where I can't think of anything but her; so I applied even more pressure but that damned will of hers won't let her break . . ." Bleakly he said: "You told me once that love hurts and I just could not understand why. Love had never hurt me. Now I know that it was because I had never been in love. Now that I am – you are right. It hurts like hell." Taking her hand: "Forgive the selfish shit I once was."

"Oh, my poor James," Corrine said plangently. It was the end of an era.

"I swear to you, I just had not the slightest idea . . ."

"You always gave full value and never promised what you could not give. We all knew what the score was – you made us read the rules first."

He winced. "God, don't remind me." His voice was

impeded when he asked: "What am I to do, Corrine? How do I break that iron will of hers? It's strapped to her back like those boards the Victorians used to make girls wear to straighten their carriage. Something has her so scared she will tote it for ever rather than take the risk of taking it off."

"Like I just said, you could try telling her."

A harsh laugh. "She would never believe me – not only does she suspect my motives she suspects my morals, and if you hold them up to the light they show up as pretty threadbare."

Corinne extracted the nugget from the grains. "You are not absolutely sure that she would welcome A Declaration, right?"

"After what I have said and done? She would send me packing and that scares the hell out of me. With the others, there was always another a long in a minute. There will never be another Harriet."

Corrine looked at him before sighing exasperatedly. "Love has indeed addled your brains. Harriet looked as she did tonight because she is walking on knives! I heard what she asked, you know, and your reply. You are the only one who can stop her committing suttee on the pyre of her pride because her reason for doing it is that she is sure all you want is another notch on your belt. She told me so; said I was not to look for her on the roll of the honoured laid—"

James gave a shout of laughter. "That's my girl," he exulted proudly. "Straight for the jugular."

"Then stitch up the wound before you both bleed to death. Make her an offer before she offers herself up as a sacrifice." Corinne paused. "Would it help if I did a little proselytising?"

Hope blazed. "Would you?"

"For the both of you, I am willing to give it another try. I'm American. We demand happy endings."

But when she called Harriet early next morning it was to be told Miss Hilliard had left town. No, she had left no forwarding address, and no, Annie could not say when Miss Hilliard would be back.

Reporting back to James he said at once: "Something is up, and my instincts tell me it is because your housewarming triggered off the explosion I was hoping for. Thanks, Corinne, but it is my job now, and the first thing to do is see Piers."

But Piers was not at home either, nor at the bank, and when James went round to Pont Street it was to find that Annie had no idea where Harriet was either, because she had not been told. "She said she had to go away for a few days, that was all, but she did not say where and she did not say when she would be back."

"Then did she leave a telephone number?"

"No, Mr Alexander, I'm afraid she did not. All she said was that she would be in touch."

So on the Monday morning James was at the shop as soon as it opened for business, where Miss Judd told him a similar story, which reinforced his conviction that there had indeed been an explosion. If Harriet had left her precious other-half without appointing a Guardian then there had to have been a divorce.

And that night, Piers turned up on James' doorstep in Cadogan Square, awash with scotch and self-pity, unshaven and bleary-eyed after forty-eight hours on the trot, to tell James the truth he suspected. On arriving back in London after the housewarming, Harriet had told him she could not become his wife.

159

She confessed to having done him wrong, but told him that if she married him she would be compounding that wrong. She had used him, she said, and for that she was both ashamed and penitent, but she was no longer able to go on lying to him – worse, lying to herself.

"Wouldn't be moved . . . couldn't shake her, pleaded and pleaded but she wouldn't give in; said she should have told me ages ago, when she first realised. Said it had nothing to do with the waiting except that if she had really loved me she would have moved heaven and hell to set me free a long time ago . . . taken on Paula and won. 'That's how I knew I didn't love you', she said. 'Only used you as something to hide behind'. Those were her exact words. I know. I've been thinking of nothing else ever since she said them to me."

And drinking to try and drown them, James thought, taking Piers into the kitchen, where he set about making some very black coffee, but exultant rather than pitying because Harriet had done it! Unstrapped herself from that damned board. Now he had to find her and give her the support he knew she would badly need. "Where has she gone?" he asked.

"Don't know . Didn't even know she'd gone 'til I went round to the flat to try and change her mind and Annie told me she'd gone away . . ." Maudlin with misery: "I accused her of having met someone else but she said that was not why she couldn't marry me . . ." Piers' red-rimmed eyes peered at James short-sightedly. He was not wearing his horn-rims. "Thought it was you – know how you are with women – so I told her she that if it was you she was wasting her time; that

160

the real reason I had brought you in was so you would buy *Harriet Designs*. Told her I hated that damned shop; took far too much of her time . . . and you were looking to set up on your own after Lewisohn's . . . told her you only agreed to help out to get the feel of the business, see if it was worth what I told you it was . . ."

Shit! thought James, closing his eyes at his own stupidity. No wonder she took flight. "And what was her reaction?"

"Said you were the last person she'd ever sell her business to. That she'd always suspected you had an ulterior motive. That was why she'd never trusted you. 'Too fly by half' were her very words. Then she said," and here Piers' voice was filled with disbelief. " 'The plain truth is that it is dead. Let us bury it decently' . . ." Piers shook his head, still having trouble assimilating it until his face crumpled in a surge of self-pity. "S'all my fault . . . I let it drag on far too long . . ."

"Yes, you did," James said brutally. "If you had really wanted Harriet you would have lit a fire under Paula years ago. It was not Harriet you were protecting from scandal and gossip; it was yourself. You just could not stand the thought of all that tabloid gossip proclaiming to the world that you had been cuckolded. The truth is that your dread of publicity was greater than your love for Harriet. Deep down you always knew that she was too much for you. Oh, you admired her and envied her but she frightened you too, didn't she? All that single-mindedness and too clever by half."

Piers mouth dropped and he turned a blustering, turkey-cock red, but the way he avoided the penetrating mercurial gaze confirmed every word James had said, as well as the fact that he was not willing to admit it.

"It is of no use you crying into your spilt milk; it has all gone down the drain and Harriet with it. But cheer up; you have still got your precious reputation. You will be able to have your no-fault divorce without so much as a mention in the gossip columns. I should have thought you would have been positively jubilant!"

Piers knew what that kind withering sarcasm meant. James was angry. So he beat a hasty retreat. Never mind the black coffee. It was sympathy he had come looking for but he was damned if he was going to hang around for blame. And it was *not* his fault. He had only wanted to protect Harriet. All he had done had been for her. All right, so he did not relish the thought of being the subject of gossip but what was wrong with that pray? He departed in high dudgeon, but James did not even see him go. He was far too deep in thought.

Ten

H arriet was in Birmingham. Her confession to
Piers had been not only the result of a long-
smoulder ending in spontaneous combustion, but a
catharsis from which she emerged purged but emotionally exhausted. Even though she knew there were
still unresolved conflicts to be sorted and solved they
would have to wait; she was too desperately tired,
caused not only by the seismic release of energy in the
form of tension her honesty had produced, but from
too many sleepless nights. She fell into bed and sleep as
if poleaxed, only to be awoken at ten minutes to eight
by an urgent telephone call from the nursing home.
Her mother had somehow managed to get hold of a
litre of whisky which she had drunk in a very short
time, resulting in unconsciousness which had now
become a coma. Harriet was advised to come at once.
She was in her car within fifteen minutes but when she
ran into Reception it was to find that her mother had
died not half an hour before without having regained
consciousness.

Harriet had the feeling she was being ground between two giant millstones. They say things come in
threes, she thought, as she sat, numbly and dumbly, in
a chair in Dr Wilson's office. First of all the realisation
that James Alexander had brought to life a sexuality

she had not realised existed, second Piers' confirmation of her suspicion that everything James said and did had an ulterior motive – not the one she thought, no, nothing so unimportant as that; his aim was the acquisition of her heart's blood – no, what *was* her heart's blood. And now this.

"Your mother was well aware of the consequences of what she did," Dr Wilson was saying. "She knew the risks involved in ingesting such an enormous quantity of alcohol in so short a time. We had taken what we thought was every precaution to prevent her getting her hands on even a tiny amount, but alcoholics become very clever at obtaining supplies, and your mother knew all the tricks. We think she must have had this particular bottle of whisky hidden where only she knew, hoarding it against the time when she could use it to accomplish her purpose."

Harriet raised her head to look at him. "Purpose?"

Dr Wilson nodded. "Her concern for you was what kept her going, but I think that once she knew you were – in her eyes – once and for all safe, in that you had learned her lessons, scaled the heights and knew better than to allow yourself to be incarcerated in the high security jail she believed marriage to be, there was no point in going on."

After a moment Harriet said slowly. "When I was here last week she made a point of telling me how proud she was because I had done everything she had urged me to do. She said it redeemed her life . . ." The doctor's face blurred as her eyes filled and she caught her breath on a stab of pain. "It never occurred to me that it was her way of saying goodbye." Too late,

Harriet saw that her mother's uncharacteristic admission had been a valediction.

"Everything your mother believed was filtered through her own experience, her own impotent rage and pain, and loving you as she did, her most desperate wish was for you to avoid what she regarded as a trap, even to brainwashing you into regarding it as such. She sent you away at an early age deliberately so that you would have no choice but to stand on your own two feet. When she saw the pictures of the house you have just done in Gloucestershire – oh yes, she showed the magazine to everybody she could buttonhole – I have never seen her so exultant – exalted, even. "She has done it", she told us. "Nobody can touch her now. She is safe, safe". When she was found she was clutching the magazine to her and there was such a smile on her face . . ."

Harriet's strained nerves broke down completely and the doctor let her weep. After that he gave her a pill and saw that she was put to bed for twelve hours.

Over the next few days she went through the funeral arrangements in a blur of grief and guilt, scrupulously carrying out her mother's instructions to the letter. "I want to be cremated", she had insisted to Harriet. "Don't bury me beside *him*. I want nothing to do with *him* in death either".

Such undying hatred, Harriet thought at the simple service. So corrosive to the spirit, so destructive to the child I was. You did a good job on me, Mother. No wonder I bound myself to *Harriet Designs*. I was far too young to understand that *your* marriage was what was wrong, not marriage in general. By the time I was old enough to realise, the damage was done; my doubts set in stone, my whole emotional structure warped and twisted. Piers was custom-made for me. It took James Alexander to come along and put his foot right through the whole rickety edifice.

After the funeral, at which she was touched to find many of the staff at the nursing home were present, plus, of course, Mrs McBride, she curled up on the sofa in her mother's house, every bar of the electric fire turned to high, and though she was wrapped in her quilted dressing gown and had draped a rug over her knees, she could not thaw the bone-piercing chill that enveloped her. Life seemed to have stranded her in an arctic landscape bereft of all human warmth and comfort. Never had she felt so alone; never had she longed so much for the warmth, strength and tenderness of James Alexander.

Several times she found her hand straying to her bag where her mobile phone lay; every time she put it back under the rug. She could not even beg for help. Even now her mother's baleful influence prevailed. Added to which had she not been right about him? It was not her he had wanted; it was *Harriet Designs*.

I had him dead to rights from the start, she thought, finding no comfort in it. He and Piers cooked up a nice little plot, except she knew who the chef was. Piers could not even boil water. Why couldn't James have been honest? There was no need to try and soften me up. But that, of course, was the way he worked, sex appeal being his stock in trade. He knew only too well that a woman was so much more amenable post-coitally. Except he never got that far with me. That was her only satisfaction, even though she knew that had he really put his mind to it that night, she would not have been able to stop him.

So . . . she sighed heavily, where do I go from here? The last thing she wanted was to return to her 'Eyes down, blinkers on' mode of existence. That life had died with her mother. No; what she needed, she decided, was a fresh start, somewhere new and totally different. And far away. America? She had been approached more than once to set up over there, but Piers had not been keen. What he wanted did not matter now since he was no longer in the picture. She had nobody to please but herself. I'll do it! she thought on a rising note of hopeful expectation. I'll slough off the old skin, sell the chrysalis to James Alexander and take nothing with the new me except my talent. I did it once; I can do it again. I have the talent and the capabilities. Use them, and take with you as much money as you can screw out of that double-crossing bastard! One way or another he will pay for his pleasure.

Having made the decision, she slept surprisingly well, and before she could change her mind drove into Birmingham next morning to see the solicitor she had retained to handle her mother's affairs; instructing him to sell the house after checking on current asking prices. She arranged to have it cleared, once she had sorted through it, its contents given to one of the charities which helped the homeless. Then she rang her own, London solicitor and told him she was selling her business and to get in touch with a Mr James Alexander, whose telephone number she gave, with whom he was to negotiate the purchase of what was a very going concern. Mr Alexander was very much

167

interested and money was no problem where he was concerned. Which was why she named a six-figure price. No, Mr Cayzer was not to be involved in the sale. That partnership was now dissolved.

Still carried along on a wave of resolution she next went into a travel agent and booked a flight to New York – from Manchester rather than London because there was less chance of meeting anyone she knew there, but as always, life had other ideas, because as she was leaving Thomas Cook she ran into someone who exclaimed: "Now there's a surprise! What you doin' up 'ere, ducks?"

It was Bert Kaye.

"Doin' a job, are yer? I'm payin' me fortnightly visit to my salon. Got so much business they can't cope so I'm opening a second one. Needless to say, the job's yours."

"I'm going abroad Bert – for quite some time."

His dismay was all but palpable. "But you're me good luck piece – if you'll pardon the expression. I ain't 'ad a salon designed by nobody but you and every one 'as turned out to be worth its weight in gold! You wouldn't let one of your very first clients down now, would yer?"

Harriet looked into his hurt face and saw his point. "Well . . . I suppose one last job . . ." He had been a very good client, thrown a lot of work her way, and she knew the drill by heart, having performed it six times already. Once the designs were done, materials ordered, Miss Judd and Evelyn could see the job through.

"I knew you wouldn't let me down. It'll only be a question of measurements and such 'cos the colours and style is always the same – my signature, like. I've

168

found the right spot so once I've signed the lease I'll call into the shop and let you know, okay?"

"I shan't be there, I'm afraid. I'm going on a trip . . . New York. Tell you what – when you are ready to proceed, why don't you call Annie, my housekeeper. She will pass on any messages to me."

If he was surprised that she said to use Annie instead of Miss Judd he did not show it. Instead he beamed and bussed her soundly. "You're a doll! Now I gotta dash – plane to catch. Ta-ta."

Having metaphorically burned all her boats, that night Harriet called Annie and gave her a list of the clothes she wished her to pack and send on, along with her passport, exhorting her to tell no one where she was. That done, she spent the next few days sorting through and packing up her mother's house, keeping what she wanted and seeing the rest go without regret. She let Mrs McBride have her pick before it did, and when the house was down to the bare boards, left it without so much as a backward glance at the man erecting the For Sale sign. That part of her life was over. Calling in on the estate agents who would be handling the sale, she handed over the keys.

On returning to her hotel, where she would be staying until she flew to New York, she called Annie again to tell her that the two cases she had packed had arrived safely, especially the one containing her all important Filofax, which contained telephone numbers and addresses vital to her commercial future, and gave her the address and telephone number of the Carlyle Hotel, (the only one she knew since Piers had always stayed there) where she would be living until she found an apartment. Annie had agreed to stay on at Pont Street until Harriet knew what was what as regards her future situation.

"There are a lot of people wanting to know where you are," Annie told her.

"Such as?"

"Well, Mr Cayzer calls practically every hour on the hour and Mr Alexander has been round every day to ask if you have been in touch."

"Keep on telling them both that you have no fresh information," Harriet instructed. "And not a word about New York to anyone, do you understand?" She had no doubt that Piers had gone in hand-wringing desperation to the man he regarded as his Good Samaritan. Pharisee, more like! was Harriet's opinion. I've taken away Piers' teaspooon and dynamited the Rock of Gibraltar. I sincerely hope, Mr Alexander, that you get clobbered by the falling rubble!

She then called Miss Judd, saying she would be away for a while and asked her to hold the fort. She did not say where she was going, only that it concerned future commissions (which was true, after all) nor did she tell her she was selling; she would not do that until she knew for sure that the sale was secure. Neither Miss Judd nor Evelyn would object to the new owner – and Harriet's conditions of sale included one that made it plain they went with the shop – for both were fervent members of the James Alexander fan club. As it was, in Harriet's opinion he would be damned lucky to get them.

The day she was due to fly to New York was a miserable day which started with grey skies, went on through drizzle and finally arrived at a downpour, but

170

she still went to the Garden of Remembrance at the crematorium. She had ordered a stone; plain black basalt bearing the name CHARLOTTE HILLIARD 1948–1998, and it was now in place. In front of it, in the urn which matched the stone, she placed a large arrangement of her mother's favourite flower, white roses. There you are, Mother, she told her silently. A long way away from Father even in death. He was buried in the cemetary at Edgbaston. His wife had never once visited his grave and Harriet had known better than to tell her that she had done so every time she came to Birmingham. In the days before her mother's funeral she had gone again, and noting that it was beginning to look neglected, made arrangements with the cemetary authorities for it to be tidied and kept that way. There was no stone, her mother having refused to do anything that would make a remembrance of her husband's life, so Harriet had arranged for one when she ordered her mother's; the same black basalt with his name FREDERICK HILLIARD 1938–1986. She had left flowers there too.

Stepping back from her mother's stone to see how the flowers looked, Harriet thought: it was not death which parted you two, it was life. The one you endured together. You should have let each other go. Other people got out of their miserable marriages. I dare say you stayed in yours because of me and because in your circle people did not get divorced; it was a social stigma. Besides, Father provided the financial security we needed. He was a good graphic designer and a talented artist in his own right: it is from him I have inherited my own talents because you had none. Which fact you never ceased to bemoan. Even if you did go straight from your father's house to that of your husband you could have acquired skills if you were so desperate. Why didn't you? There were always night classes. But you always blamed him for trapping you, as you saw it, even though it was as much your fault; it takes two to quarrel after all. If you had left him you would have had no one to blame but yourself for any failures. It was easier to stay and blame him. It took an intuitive and perceptive man to show me a different perspective, and for that at least, I am grateful to him. I see the whole picture now, not just your re-painted corner. I also understand a great deal more about myself. Enough to know that next time I meet a man who strikes a chord I will not lock up my instrument.

Opening her umbrella she turned to go, only to look straight into the Waterman's ink-blue eyes of James Alexander. He was standing just outside the railings of the Garden of Remembrance, regarding her with an unsmiling face. His dark hair was a-glitter with rain and he looked tired and unshaven, his hands thrust deep into the pockets of his Burberry. Harriet was willing to bet they were clenched. What right have *you* to be angry? she thought bitterly, a spurt of her own giving her the impetus to walk towards him.

"So you are a Brummie," he opened, as she reached him.

"What are you doing here?" Harriet stood back and admired her own coolness.

"Waiting for you, of course."

"If it is about the sale of *Harriet Designs* my lawyer is handling everything. I have a plane to catch."

"I don't give a damn about your *alter ego* or your plane. We have unfinished business, you and."

172

"We have nothing to discuss – my lawyer has all the details. Talk to him."

"Don't be obtuse, Harriet. It's not your style." Before she knew what he was about he had an unshakeable grip on her elbow and was leading her purposefully in the direction of the car park.

"Now wait a minute—"

"No more minutes, I have waited quite long enough."

She had to trot to keep up with his long strides, which was what probably made her sound breathless when she asked: "For what?"

"You know very well for what."

Which perversely made her dart down a side-turning. "How did you find me?"

"By leaving no stone unturned – but ultimately by running into Bert Kaye, who told me he had seen you in Birmingham, and that you were going abroad. Your solicitor's telephone call was the second clue but he refused to tell me where you were. So on a hunch I turned to the Birmingham telephone directories and called every damned Hilliard in the book. (Thank God your name isn't Smith!) None of them were the Hilliard I was looking for but one of them had been disconnected even though their number was still in the book, so I acted on my hunch and came up, only to find – once I found the house – that there was a For Sale sign up. I was about to turn tail and head for the estate agent when a very loquacious lady named Mrs McBride came out of next door, and she very helpfully filled me in on the whys and wherefores of the Hilliards, who used to live at 147 Amberley Close."

His voice all but undid her when he went on: "I am

173

so sorry about your mother. When Mrs McBride told me about the cremation I took a chance I might find you here."

But Harriet was in a daze. He had come looking for her! Her, Harriet Hilliard NOT *Harriet Designs*. The implications were so far-reaching she could not seem to get a grip on them. She could only go with the flow – and it was going in his direction. On reaching his car he opened the front passenger door before plucking the umbrella from her unnerved hand, giving her no choice but to get in out of the now heavy rain. She did so, and sat there in a bemused state listening to the drum of the rain on the roof and watching the raindrops trickling down the windscreen. Closing her umbrella he tossed it onto the back seat before going round to the driver's side.

"Now, let's get a few things straight, shall we?" he began pleasantly, but in a voice that indicated a very short end of tether. "For a start, I am not and never have been interested in buying your shop."

"But Piers said—"

"The wrong thing, as usual. It was his idea to unload it, not mine. He thought – and for once he was right – that it was taking you over; receiving the attention he felt you should be lavishing on him, and wanted me to use your business to get a foot in the door with the object of acquiring it. That was why he was so eager to bring me in. He had not the slightest idea you were giving your all to it because it meant far more to you than he did, or that you clung to it so fiercely because you had nothing else."

Harriet said nothing. She had wondered how he had penetrated her disguise; now she was about to find out.

He went on: "I know all about you now, Harriet, thanks to your nosy neighbour, and I think I have completed the crossword. If I get any of the answers wrong no doubt you will set me straight in your own, inimitable way."

Harriet still said nothing, not only uncertain of what she should say but content to wait on events.

"I am often wrong," James went on, "but I was right about you. The first time I met you I thought you had the kind of face which not only compelled a man's eyes but was of the kind that causes him to wonder what is going on behind it; only to realise that Piers had never once wondered as much – worse, the idea had never so much as entered his mind. He took you at your face value which, I have to tell you, is considerable, but was content to leave it at that. Oh, you were very — got-together, but in my experience people so conspicuously in control of every aspect of their lives are usually terrified of what might happen if they let go. It also intrigued me mightily as to what a woman like you was doing with a man like Piers, to whom control means one thing only: financial regulation. So I decided to find out. You see, when Piers first sang your praises – a veritable *Te Deum*, I might add – my first reaction was a groan and a 'Here's another fine mess he's got himself into', but this time with a much more subtle and devious woman, until, on meeting you, I realised that it was not his money you were after. On the contrary I discovered – and not through Piers either – that you had worked like a beaver to repay every penny he had ever lent you. So why, I wondered, was a woman with your capability and drive happy to allow an unresolved situation to drift on aimlessly, making

175

no attempt to steer for the shore, until it came to me that it suited you; that if you never saw land again you would be quite content. Being the kind of man who likes his questions answered, I decided I would do as Piers asked, since it offered me the perfect cover for six weeks digging into the whys and wherefores of Harriet Hilliard. It was when you got all steamed up at what you termed my 'interference' that I knew I had been right about you. I can recognise panic when I see it."

Harriet could not repress a quiver.

At once he asked: "Cold?" Taking her hands: "Like ice. Never mind, Harriet, the thaw is about to set in . . ." He moved then, in that great-cat way of his, opening first his damp Burberry then his jacket, so that he could pull her right against the warmth of his body and put his arms around her. "Go on," he commanded. "Put your arms around me."

Harriet obeyed him meekly, for once in her life not in the least inclined to argue.

"That's better . . . now you can stop pouring cement into that stiff upper lip."

Harriet closed her eyes. Here was the warmth and physical contact for which she had yearned, and not only the physical reality. She could feel the heat he was generating melting the icy shell into which she had been locked for so long, and when he gathered her close in a way that made his feelings for her plain, put his cheek to her bright hair, she sighed once and felt her tension seep away, leaving her all limp with longing.

"How is that lip anyway?" He raised her chin with a forefinger. "No scar, but let's just make sure it is in good working order, shall we?" His kiss was so sweetly tender, so loving, that she felt tears prick even as her own mouth clung, admitting her own feelings. "You see . . . no lasting effects."

"That's all you know . . ."

He grinned. "That's better. You will be glad to know you have just confirmed my theory."

"About what?"

"Us. That your effect on me is matched only by my effect on you. I have not been losing sleep and chasing clues this past week just because I don't like loose ends. I've been doing it because you *are* my end, not to mention its beginning, plus the rest of my life."

Slowly, as if afraid of what she would see, Harriet raised her head, looked into his eyes. They were deeply blue and she knew what that meant. It was when they were black and glittery that they unnerved her. She let loose a luxurious sigh. "If only you knew how much I have longed to hear you say that. I felt so alone and I wanted and needed you so much."

"Say again."

"I needed – need – and want you so much. You brought me out of hibernation; aroused feelings in me I had not known I possessed, feelings that were stronger than my ability to contain them. In the end, I found that I did not want to." It was said shyly but it was said.

"There! It was not so hard to say, was it? Everyone needs someone, Harriet. Why should you be different?"

"Because I was conditioned to be."

"Ah . . ." he said, sounding like the man who has just seen Sesame Open. "Tell me," he invited, in a way that made it plain he wanted to know because it was as important to him as it was to her; that everything about her was important to him.

So she told him about her mother. She told him everything, in fact, right down to the time when, on meeting an old friend of Piers, she had found him so overwhelmingly attractive that she had fearfully and instinctively channelled that attraction into dislike, terrified to stray so much as an inch from her mother-constructed straight and narrow, yet still ending up on the rocks of forlorn hopes. "I am so glad you came looking for me," she finished, her voice muffled against the crisp cotton of his shirt.

"Not half as glad as I am that I found you. You had better know right now that I am a very persistent man when I want something."

This time what she said was even more muffled,

Tipping her chin again: "Don't be afraid to say it to my face," he encouraged.

"I asked – what is it you want?"

His smile made her quiver. "You are being uncharacteristically obtuse – or is it that you are at last learning to act like a female? Using feminine wiles?"

"I am not sure I know how. I was never taught any."

"Never mind. Whatever you are – or are not – it is what I want." He pinned her with his brilliant eyes. "Know this, Harriet. I am in love with you. I am in love as I never thought I would love anyone. I think you are in love with me, but I would very much like to hear you say so."

Harriet took a deep breath and committed herself once and for all. "Yes, I love you. I love you as I never thought to love anyone. The more I got to know you the more I loved you. That's what had me running

178

scared. You see, I had got it into my head that all you wanted was another notch on your belt."

"I threw that away – see." He opened his arms so that she could see the leather belt around his waist. "Not a notch to be seen on this brand new one."

"I was still convinced you were only on one of your recruiting drives."

"Actually, I never needed to recruit," he told her with a staight face. "There were always plenty of volunteers . . ."

Harriet giggled, then stated rather than asked: "You've have had a lot of women, haven't you?"

"Put them down to practice until the real thing came along. But you are not going to hold my past against me. I hope?"

"The only thing I expect you to hold in future is me."

"Done!"

This time the silence was longer, broken only by rustlngs and murmurs and the sound of kisses, until Harriet asked: "And Rina?"

"What about her?"

"She won't take this lying down?

"Why not? It is the only way she ever takes anything. Rina, my sweet innocent, is Casanova's female equivalent. She has left more men for dead than I have had hot dinners. Our brief fling had a great deal of physical content but neither of us packed our emotions. Love had nothing to do with it. On the other hand, where you are concerned, love has every thing to do with it . . ." The way he kissed her proved it. "By the time I am done with you, Harriet, you will have got rid of every one of those brainwashed inhibitions of yours. You have such a lot to learn, my love. How lucky I am to be the man who will have the pleasure of teaching you." And after a while he sighed luxuriously before complimenting: "And how quickly you learn . . ."

But Harriet wanted all her ghosts exorcised. "Like Rina?"

"I can see I shall have to set your doubts at rest once and for all about Rina. The first time I kissed you I knew you had feelings for me from the way you responded; you seared my nerve ends like a flame – but I could also see they shocked and scared you. I needed something which which to prise you loose from whatever it was that had your emotions under lock and key, so I decided to add a soupçon of jealousy. I have never known it to fail. I took Rina to Bermuda expressly for that purpose, even though our *affaire* was in its dying fall. I was impatient and wanted to stir things up but most of all I wanted to stir you up. I desperately wanted you to think of me the way I had come to think of you – to the exclusion of everyone and everything else. After all, my first attempt never got off the ground."

Harriet looked up at him. "First attempt?"

"When I persuaded Charles to let me drive you over to Sheringham Court, hoping to get you alone and make some inroads into those self-defences of yours, only you seized on Jeremy as cover; worse, the whole thing went pear-shaped when you fell down those cellar steps. When I kissed you that night, I honestly meant to do no more than comfort you after your nightmare, but again your response was such that I threw caution to the winds, mistakenly let loose my ravenous appetite for you and stampeded you into running back to Piers. So I decided to go for broke by taking Rina to Bermuda where I knew Paula was, and tackle her too. It was the action of a desperate man, but when I saw you at Corinne's house-party, though I knew I had succeeded I felt guilty as hell. You were obviously held together by sheer force of will, but at the same time I knew that I had no alternative if I was to stop you digging away at your own grave, with Piers standing by convinced it was only a flower bed!"

"Jeremy told me you had told him that was what I was doing."

James smiled. "Did he indeed."

Harriet eyed him. "You knew he would tell me, didn't you?"

"I hoped he would. I've just told you. I was desperate."

"Well your stratagem worked. I was eaten up with jealousy, not to mention envy, even though I was convinced that you now were testing me; making sure I was up to Piers and not just another Paula."

"Up to him! My dear, sweet Harriet you were always far too much for him. You are, however, absolutely perfect for me. It was because of you that I spent time with a woman who was already bored with me and casting her lures elsewhere".

"It was what you told me – or rather asked me; why not? That really did it for me. Because when I forced myself to answer your question honestly I knew I could not go on shying away from the truth, and that the sooner I told it to Piers the better. Once I had told him – and it was not easy, believe me, because I had to hurt him – I knew I had done the right thing because I felt as though a ton weight had been lifted from my shoulders. Only next morning they called about my mother . . ."

"My poor sweet." James pulled her closer to him.

"She only ever wanted the best for me, really."

James, who had been appalled as well as enlightened by the litany of emotional abuse to which Harriet had been subjected said thoughtfully: "Philip Larkin was dead right when he said – and I think I am quoting correctly: *'life can take so long to climb/Clear of its wrong beginnings, and may never . . .'*, You, my love have climbed clear."

"Thanks to you."

Something in Harriet's voice had him sighing drolly: "Go on, say it. Fancy a man like you quoting poetry."

Harriet shook her head. "Why shouldn't you? You can do everything else."

"Oh, such faith – what have I done to deserve it?" His voice was light but his eyes showed how much her words meant to him.

"I will tell you when we have nothing else to do on long winter nights," Harriet promised mischeviously.

"Where we are concerned there will *always* be something we can do no matter what the season, night or day, and I can't wait to get started. Mind you, we shall doubtless knock a few corners off each other, because I am no Piers, I do not believe in the old 'anything to please', adage. If it does not please me, I say so. You, on the other hand, please me inordinately. I have no doubt that there will be times when we shall argue uphill and down dale – especially about *Harriet Designs* – but a wrangle with you is equivalent to a hypo of pure adrenalin! You have no idea how I missed our verbal stand-offs."

182

"*You* did!" Harriet exclaimed. Then: "You *really* don't want to buy me out?"

"Nope. Never did. I only went along with the idea because it provided the perfect cover. However, in view of all that has happened since, how does a partnership strike you?"

"Dumb," Harriet replied faintly.

"Never! I rather thought you enjoyed working with me."

"I loved it! We struck sparks . . . you made work fun again . . ."

"Then let's strike some more."

"Oh, yes – yes please!"

"Just so long as you are quite sure about your divorce from the other Harriet. I have no intention of aiding and abetting you to commit bigamy."

"I have already instituted proceedings."

James' smile bathed her. "You are a desiging woman, Harriet Hilliard, in more ways than one."

"Well, I had designs on you from the moment I set eyes on you, though without being aware of it. It was what had me working myself into the ground to try and sublimate it."

"I know."

Harriet sat up to look at him. "Just how did you suss me out so quickly?"

"I told you. I am experienced enough to know when I strike a certain kind of response from a woman and yours to me the first time we met told me one thing but hinted tantalisingly at another." He kissed her again. "So I made up my mind to find out what that was. It's a good job I did, don't you think?"

"Around you I don't think as well as I should . . ."

"Likewise. Around you I have this urge to do, rather than think . . ." James proceeded to demonstrate.

Coming up for air Harriet said shakily: "Just remember that this new woman is still being run in. You, on the other hand, have an awful lot of mileage. You will give me the benefit of your expertise, won't you?"

The blue eyes held a gleam that sent her expectations soaring. "Will I? That, my first and last love, is the understatement of this or any other century." Bending his head to hers again: "Here beginneth the first lesson . . ."